Transformation through 'Thinking' Positive

AF522495

Other books by Author

Transformation through 'Thinking' Positive

Dr. Ashutosh Karnatak

PRABHAT
PAPERBACKS

No part of this publication can be reproduced, stored in a retrieval system or transmitted in any form or by any means, electronic, mechanical, photocopying, recording or otherwise, without the prior permission of the author and the publisher.

Published by
PRABHAT PAPERBACKS
4/19 Asaf Ali Road,
New Delhi-110 002 (INDIA)
e-mail: prabhatbooks@gmail.com

ISBN 978-93-5322-754-8
TRANSFORMATION THROUGH 'THINKING' POSITIVE
by Dr. Ashutosh Karnatak

Edition
First, 2020

Price
₹ 250.00 (Rupees Two Hundred Fifty only)

© Reserved

Printed at
R-Tech Offset Printers, Delhi

Renovate, Innovate, Reinvent self
by
'Thinking' Positive

"Life is a Marathon,
Here, neither fatigue nor stoppage is allowed
Rise, Walk, Run, Fall down and again Rise or Crawl
Don't stop till you get the desired objective."

"Gone are the days to walk and even run, it's a time to fly"

(Book on transforming self by Dr Ashutosh Karnatak after Success of 'Yes, You Can')

Foreword

Positive thinking, it is said, is highly contagious. Anyone who is acquainted with Dr. Asuthosh Karnatak needs no proof. He is always bubbling with energy, new ideas and meets his targets before time. Needless to say, his book on positive thinking comes more out of his experience and conviction that thinking positive is the sure key to success and happiness.

The book begins with the virtues of positive thinking and explains the philosophy behind this virtue. In other words, be it a individual, organisation or the entire country, the need to adopt "can do" attitude becomes a primary step for success.

Positive thinking is also an essential ingredient for achieving success in any endeavour. Ascendency in our personal, official and social life is paved with various steps and hurdles. No one is spared of these steps and it has never been a hurdle-free path for those who have reached the apex of success. Lady luck's smiles and favourable circumstances are but excuses that losers give to gloss over their setback. What matters the most is the positive attitude towards the task on hand, be it a personal one or an office assignment or working towards a goal.

As a social being human life is seamlessly connected at various levels with other individuals. This social connect determines the contours of our individual and social behaviour.

This is the reason why we find change in people's behaviour as individuals and while in a group. It is in this behavioural pattern that positivity is reflected differently from that of negativity or the lack of positivity.

The lack of positivity results in lack of self confidence. This in turn results in low self-esteem that reflects in the thinking process, effort and output. Fall in output reflects in the loss of an organisation and sets the process of slide while failure in a individual leads to high levels of stress, frustration, anger and negativity.

This could explain the reasons for the success and failure, high and low productivity and winners and losers being set apart. This is what the author calls 'the maha mantra of success'.

Our ancient scriptures abound in messages, literally pathways to success through positive attitude in every walk of life. No situation can be an impediment in progress if one adopts the dictum "this too will pass" (*etad api gamishyati*). As is said in Mahabharata, *charanmarganvijaanati* (one who starts walking finds the path).

Scientific temper and innovative minds are probably the best examples positivity and a 'never give up' attitude, the urge to learn from mistakes, make errors and failures verily the stepping stone to success.

The book cogently explains the attributes of positivity in life and the working process in an organisation for which the author deserves all praise.

Those who have made this country great are the ones who are endowed with the quality of positive thinking, as Dr. Karnatak very rightly elucidates in his book. Wish this quality found in a few becomes truly contagious at the shortest possible time.

—Seshadri Chari

Contents

Introduction

'Positivity leads to possibilities, which, in turn, give birth to options. Options pave the way to solutions. Thus positivity transforms problems into solutions. This is the first theorem of positivity.'

The most important wealth of any country or a company is its human resource, for example, Japan, as a country, has almost no natural resource but it still is one of the most advanced countries on this planet. The reason – its citizens!!

During the long journey of my professional career, my interaction with a wide range of people – young, old, from different strata of society and varied cultures have led me to believe that countries could have sustainable development on the basis of a positive framework of the society.

India, one of the youngest countries in the world, can also become a prosperous country if our youth power is utilised positively. ***By 2020, the average age in India will be 29 years and it is set to become the world's youngest country with 64 % of its population in the working-age group.*** Today, every fifth person in India is an adolescent (10-19 years) and every third, a young person (10-24 years).

Countries like Western Europe, the USA, South Korea, Japan, and China have grown rich before they could grow old by investing in education and skills, health, empowerment, and employment. India should also invest in the betterment of its youth by developing winnable attributes. It will pay rich dividends if the youth of India are empowered with synchronised vision, competencies and Thinking Positive to help in the growth of the country.

As a nation of one-and-a-quarter billion people, India needs to gear up against the numerous challenges that it faces in social, political, economic, geographical and other arenas. Though India has made substantial progress since independence, in spite of certain shortcomings, much still remains to be done in many different spheres.

What we all need is a change in the mindset to keep India going with greater vigor and vitality. A positive India would mark the beginning of a change in the thinking and behavior of the people. 'Catch them young' should be the mantra as behavior is easier to change in the early years of one's life.

'Positive India - Competent India - Projectised India'

Positive India

Thinking Positive is the mother of all virtues. If entire India becomes positive, much of its problems would get solved as it would unleash the true potential of this vibrant and diverse nation. In this regard, a website ***www.plusapproach.org*** is dedicated to the propagation of positive thinking amongst the masses through articles, positive stories, quotes, presentations, and other channels. Some of the direct advantages of Thinking Positive are listed below:

- Start seeing the half glass of water as 'half full' instead of 'half empty'.
- Adopt transformation to 'can do' approach.
- Always look for solutions.

'Positivity leads to possibilities, which in turn give birth to options. Options pave the way to solutions. Thus positivity transforms problems into solutions. This is the first theorem of positivity.'

Competent India

The second pillar for making a strong India is *competency building* in the population in professional areas of leadership, strategy, planning, soft skills, etc. Competency helps to enhance man's efficiency and effectiveness in achieving a given objective.

Positive India will act like a solid foundation, over which the edifice of competent India will be built on. Mind accepts and retains something for only as long as heart allows. India has got the youngest working population in the world. This demographic dividend will bear fruits if the youth has got the right skills along with right opportunities. India is blessed with and home for great sculptors, artisans, weavers, craftsmen since the ages.

On the same note, the new India has astonished the world by producing some of the finest brains in fields of Medicine, Engineering, Space Research, and Information Technology. People who are born, brought up and educated in India are making waves around the world by their sheer entrepreneurial skills. But the large portion of our population has still not been a part of this new emerging India. India needs to give competence edge especially to this population to develop in more inclusive manner.

A particular region should be modeled and recognised on the basis of its uniqueness. For instance, Moradabad is famous for brass works in India. It's time that it is made a household name in the world when it comes to products of brass. Top quality product along with first-grade marketing is required to make a mark in today's global village. If Switzerland is today known for high quality watches which are costlier than even the automobiles, it's because they have made it an object of dream. The aspirational value of the watch is much more than its real worth. And many things go in tandem with each other to make a successful product. Switzerland as a place in itself has got an aspirational value. People around the world wish to visit Switzerland. People see the things in totality. Therefore, the watch is not a watch in itself; it is a status symbol.

Overall, India needs to gear up to drive its masses out of poverty and become a truly competent nation.

'Competency helps sharpen the sword of experience.'

Projectised India

The third element over which India needs to build on is its Projectisation. It is the culmination of the other two qualities, the result part of this PI-CI-PI strategy. This will rack up the trajectory of India's growth story in perceptible terms. Positive India and Competent India will act as the groundwork for successful completion of thousands of project, as small as daily office work by an executive to as large as any billion dollar infrastructure project.

Projectised India will help develop consciousness of time, cost and quality in the citizens as these are absolutely critical to the development of this country. Every minute is a currency, which we are losing by wasting it. Projectised India will lead to progressive India. Progressive India will ultimately complement its positive and competent populace. The importance of other project-related concepts like scope, execution, control, and monitoring, not only relate to projects but to many other facets of everyone's life.

A positive attitude is compulsory to be able to identify the options and solutions and not keep struggling with the problems. To turn a person from disable to able and to a winner, a positive approach in all spheres of life is required.

Projectisation of India is required to develop time consciousness and purpose. Moreover, competency development helps to achieve the objectives efficiently and effectively.

'Excellence develops after maturity, innovation follows excellence and excellence leads to leadership.'

With this book, I have tried to touch upon the idea of Thinking Positive and how it may lead to the development of a positive society, positive India and a positive universe as a whole. The book is intended to help employ a positive approach, not only in professional life but also in day-to-day life as well. The intention to bring out this book is to disseminate positive thinking among the masses so that they can face the challenges of this competitive world happily and without stress.

Keeping the interest of general masses in view, I have tried to make the contents easy to read and comprehensible so that one can imbibe and practice them in case of any depressive moment. These can work as a positive palliative to emerge from the negative moment.

I have been following and practicing positive thinking for the last 20 years and have experienced tremendous advantages of it. I have been successful in changing the lives of many people through my talks and writings which are published in my website **www.plusapproach.org**. On seeing the response, I was encouraged to pen down my thoughts after literature survey on this subject.

Hope you will like this book and spread Positive Thinking and Thinking Positive among your acquaintances so that they are successful, happy and peaceful.

This book would be able to transform thinking process of readers, enabling them to be positive, which would pave the way of life towards success, happiness and peace.

—Dr. Ashutosh Karnatak

1

Power of Thinking Positive

"He who reigns within himself and rules his passions, desires, and fears is more than a king."

—John Milton

Power of Thinking Positive

"Life is a contract given by God,
it is up to us how we manage it"

Life is as uncertain as a drop of water on the banana leaf. Most of the time of our lives being passed in molding our self, maintaining relationships, taking care of our health, etc.

Lifetime Management

Our active life is of about 30 years, which is equivalent to 2,62,800 hours. If we work in a day for 12 hours, then our working life shall amount to 1,31,400 hours. Now, if we pass our life in wallowing in a negative attitude about 50 % of the time, the active life gets reduced to 65,700 hours, which is equivalent to 5,475 days or 15 years. So effectively, 30 years are reduced to 15 years, or our life is shortened by 15 years. If we try to improve our mental attitude at least 75 %, the span of our active life can be increased to 23 years. By a further increase in the plus position, a substantial increase in a busy life can be noticed. It is worth noting that by adopting a negative attitude, one not only reduces the active life but also invites ailments like blood pressure, stress and related diseases. So negativity, to be converted to positivity, calls for utilising our life in a most effective and efficient manner so that a successful and happy life is led without any place for whining.

'Positivity reduces the possibility of sorrow at the end of an active life.'

Positivity is nothing but a change in perspective by keeping others' positions and circumstances into consideration. It is like a converter which changes the viewpoint. Thoughts are like a virus which multiplies very fast in a medium of negativity. I remember reading that in order to nullify one negative thought, we have to build at least five positive thoughts. The moot question is whether positive thoughts can be generated or developed by practice?

Based on my own experience, positivity has a tremendous impact as it helps in bringing about **a self-positive change** by:

1 Being fearless
2 Developing a helping attitude
3 Developing empathy and forgiving attitude
4 Inspiring others
5 Laying emphasis on persuasion and perseverance
6 Limiting stress
7 Making the impossible possible
8 Reducing anger
9 Remaining active throughout the day
10 Remaining unperturbed
11 Treating every problem as a challenge

A human being is the only mammalian possessing the 'thinking' mind and this makes him different from others. This mental faculty plays an important role in life, provided it works efficiently. The word 'efficiently' is used to lay stress on 'productive thinking'. Productive thinking needs deliberate cultivation and development like when a seed is sown in fertile land, it produces a better yield than the seed sown in a barren land. Therefore, the same seed delivers different results, based on the condition of the land. In the case of human beings, this land is the 'mind'. A fertile mind will yield better thoughts, leading to better health.

What is Positive Thinking?

It is our mental attitude which reflects in our day-to-day working, as thinking is a reflection of our attitude and attitude gives rise to action.

One may ask as to how can we know if the other person thinks positive or not?

The litmus test is: ***'He always looks for solutions.'***

Apart from this, a positive-thinking person has the following attributes:

- Accepts the situation
- Always seems hopeful
- Always smiles
- Appreciates others
- Avoids getting disturbed over trivial issues
- Believes in patience, persistence, perseverance
- Decision maker
- Distress or worry does not reflect on the face
- Does multitasking
- Does not crib
- Does not get stressed
- Does not harbor prejudice
- Empathises
- Ever ready to help others
- Fearless
- Finds options
- Gratitude
- Growing mindset

- Happy disposition
- Has 'can do' approach
- Has resilience
- Healthy thoughts
- Helpful attitude
- Hopeful
- Immense confidence
- Innovative thinker
- Inspires others
- Intrinsic inspiration
- Knows better time management
- Likes challenges
- Looks for solutions
- Makes the 'impossible possible'
- More commitment towards the task on hand
- Obstacles act as challenges and opportunities
- Optimistic; invariably sees a silver lining to every cloud
- Possesses extra power to forgive and tolerate
- Possesses the desire to learn
- Sees half glass filled; not as half glass empty
- Shows an agile and flexible approach
- Unruffled with problems

Advantages of Thinking Positive

Mental Development

- A disabled person becomes enabled
- A larger area of flexibility is possible due to awareness of one's operating bandwidth
- Acts like manure for the mind, which needs to be continuously fed in order to produce healthy thoughts and ideas
- Capable of storing more information and knowledge
- Creates more mental space by activating the right brain, leading to happiness and bliss
- Develops the capacity to learn and unlearn
- Enhancement of the zone of acceptability
- Enhances free space in mind
- Finds possibilities and options to risks and obstacles
- Germinates sprouts of healthy thoughts
- Helps in the internal generation and in directing thoughts, efforts, and energy. Like a catalyst, enhances the propensity of attributes
- Increases resilience capacity
- Negative thoughts get auto-cleaned
- Positivity builds one; negativity breaks. Never allow negativity to overpower you
- Positivity is created at the workplace through a positive mental disposition
- Positivity is like a firewall that reflects or converts negative emotions into solutions or opportunities
- Positivity is like water which seeps down through the available pores. Negativity blocks the mind with negative thoughts, preventing positive thoughts from seeping in

- Purifies the soul
- Reduces noise in the mind
- Thinks about possibilities and options to counter risks and hurdles
- Widens the horizon. Makes one think beyond oneself

Emotional Development

- Develops empathy
- Develops more emotional control
- Enhances forgiveness zone and tolerance
- Prevents distress from showing on the face
- Reduces prejudice level

Capability

- A disabled person gets enabled
- Develops the ability to unlearn and relearn
- Enhances ability to bear greater pain. Initially, the pain incites one to take action to get rid of it, but gradually when one is not successful in getting rid of it, it becomes a part of life and does not bother. Again, whenever any pain of severe intensity is encountered, one knows how to deal with it and not get perturbed
- Enhances appreciation capability
- Enhances leadership skills, facilitating greater acceptance by society
- Focuses on 'can' instead of an attitude of 'can't'
- Helps in migrating from uncertainty to certainty
- Helps in migrating from uncertainty to certainty
- Looks ahead after any setback
- Power of acceptance and strength of ego counterbalance each other

Delivery

- Enhances the delivery quotient
- Helps to improve performance
- Improvement in the rate of success as determination increases

Potency of Attributes

- Enhances flexibility and acceptability
- Helps to build a parental attitude
- Increases determination, confidence, and persistence

Changes in Perception

- Changes outlook, perspective, and perception about persons, situations, and circumstances
- Enhances ownership
- Starts seeing a half glass of water as being half-filled and not half unfilled

Impact on Life

- Builds a balanced personality
- Develops enthusiasm and energy level
- Enhances internal energy
- Helps to face a crisis without getting perturbed
- Improves health, decreases stress and thereby reduces the risk of a heart attack
- Incites one to think and work for the society
- Increases optimism and happiness
- Leads to happiness, the main ingredient essential for creating harmony within self, society and the nation

Positivity and Success

Positivity has a clear co-relation with success. In fact, positivity impacts the mind, which is the nodal agency for regulating the actions of any individual. 'Desire to do' is the critical attribute for success. One may have millions of dollars or is highly competent, but if there is no or less desire to move forward, there can be no positivity.

Positivity not only develops the desire to take action but also empowers this attribute. Man, by and large, is lazy by nature. Positivity takes him out of his lethargy and activates the glands of his brain, making it release hormones like dopamine, which pushes a person to move ahead.

Someone may ask, 'Why should I be positive?' He may be happy living in the 'I am okay' syndrome. But it is also correct that unless and until one derives some benefit out of anything, one would not like to change oneself. It is only when one starts getting an advantage, one prepares to alter one's habits, behavior, and nature.

Newton, a great scientist, who derived the Law of Gravity, defined his Third Law of Motion thus: 'Every action has a reaction'.

In terms of success, when we fail, then we take action. Thus this law can be redefined as:

"Every action has a reaction and every reaction has a pro-action.

In terms of success, after every failure, we tend to repent and most of the time, we leave the objective and work towards achieving a different goal.

This pro-action occurs due to the impact of positivity, which inspires us to persevere – a valuable ingredient to achieving success besides many other attributes.

Maha-mantra of Success

Positivity helps in inner energisation and assists in directing thoughts, efforts, and energy towards our goal as these are the principal ingredients for achieving success. It helps in the application of these attributes and removes the lethargy inventory or lackadaisical attitude. It also fills one with the capacity to deliver. It is like a positive injection, which enhances the propensity of the attribute and prods one to work towards the application of the same.

Positivity makes a significant contribution to success in life, which is the prime objective of life, particularly in this competitive world with an environment of struggle.

So, Why not be positive?

Thinking Positive is nothing but a sense of perception. A very common test is the reaction to seeing a glass of water half-filled with water. One may say that it is half filled or half empty. In case the glass is filled with milk, a positive person will see the half-empty space as the strength of the glass and treat it as an opportunity to fill milk in the glass. In both cases, one sees the same empty space, but the approach is different. This is called a 'plus approach' as it sees the strength of the person, place, thing or condition.

We need to orient our minds to perceive the strength of everything, knowing well what negatives are. This does not mean that one should avoid seeing the negative aspects but one should perceive the strength of the aspects, knowing well what negatives are. The intent is to perceive the totality and presume the positive aspect of the same.

A person wants to become a positive thinker and wants to develop positivity whenever doubts arise in his or her mind. However, adverse circumstances develop that force a person to become negative. This, however, does not apply to all as reactions of different persons to the same circumstances may be different. Had it been otherwise, everyone would have reacted in the same way. Thus the myth that circumstances drive us to negativity has to be erased out of the mind and such a mental attitude be developed that one remains in control over one's thinking and state of mind.

Thus, conclusively dreams can be achieved, if they are seen with open eyes and they are Smart with your commitment and self-belief.

Nuggets

- Lead life in a most rewarding way by Thinking Positive
- Thinking Positive defines your Persona
- Develop Self positive change
- Positivity inspires perseverance to achieve success

"Success isn't a result of spontaneous combustion. You must set yourself on fire."

—Arnold H. Glasow

□

Notes

(I am being Positive)

Pen down your thoughts/experiences –

Takeaway –

2

Negative Thinking

"If you think you can, you can.
If you think you can't, you're right!"

—Mary Kay Ash

Negative Thinking and Its Impact

Negative Thinking

It is necessary to understand before we develop positivity of mind, that negative situations will be encountered in day-to-day life. If you were lowered into an MRI scanner – a huge doughnut-shaped magnet that can take a video of the neural changes occurring in the brain and flash the word 'no' for less than one second, dozens of stress-producing hormones and neurotransmitters would be released, which can be seen in the encephalograph. These chemicals immediately interrupt the normal functioning of the brain, impairing logic, reason, language processing, and communication. They begin to develop stress in the mind.

In fact, just seeing a list of negative words for a few seconds will make a highly anxious or depressed person feel worse and the more he or she delves on them, the more he or she would actually damage the key structures that regulate the memory, feelings, and emotions. The person will get disturbed sleep, loss of appetite and inability to experience long-term happiness and satisfaction.

If one were to vocalise one's negativity, or even slightly frown at the word 'no', more stress chemicals would be released not only in one's brain, but in the listener's brain as well. The listener will experience increased anxiety and irritability, thereby undermining cooperation and trust. In fact, just hanging around negative people can make you more prejudiced towards others!

Any form of negative rumination, for example, worrying about financial issues or health, can stimulate the release of destructive neurochemicals. The same holds true for children too – the more negative thoughts they have, the more likely they are to experience emotional turmoil. But if they are taught to think positively, they can turn their lives around.

Negative thoughts are enervating and drain one's energy levels. Thoughts containing words like 'never', 'should' and 'can't', complaints, whining or thoughts that lower one's sense of self-worth deplete the body by producing corresponding chemicals that weaken the physiology. No wonder the person feels exhausted at the end of the day!

The most dangerous word is 'no'.

Some negative words are:

- **Cannot do**
- **Difficult**
- **Failure**
- **Friction**
- **Impossible**
- **Not possible**
- **Pain**
- **Stress**

Negative words are time-wasters for both the speaker as well as the listener as their minds get engaged in convincing each other. It does not mean that one cannot say 'no' to anything, but the objective is to have a positive intention when taking an action.

Fear-provoking words, like poverty, illness, and death also stimulate the brain in negative ways and even if these fearful thoughts are not justified, the other parts of the brain (the thalamus and amygdala) react to negative fantasies as though they are actual threats from the outer world. Curiously, man has been hardwired to worry – perhaps inherited from memories carried over from ancestral times when there were countless threats to man's survival. We produce up to 50,000 thoughts a day and 70-80 % of them are negative. This translates into 40,000 negative thoughts a day that needs managing and filtering – no small task for any person to handle.

Even the most confident individuals fall prey to negative, judgmental, irrational, fear-based thoughts that challenge their actions and prick holes in their plans.

In order to interrupt this natural propensity to worry, several steps can be taken. First, ask yourself a question: 'Is the situation really a threat to my personal survival?' Usually, it is not and the faster you can interrupt the amygdala's reaction to an imagined threat, the quicker you can take action to solve the problem. You'll also reduce the possibility of storing a permanent negative memory in the brain.

Negativity is injurious to health: A person fails because of the negativity present within. Even if one were to induce positivity in oneself, success will not appear until positivity wins over negativity. This is because the positivity neutralises the negativity and if the positivity does not exceed negativity, the result will be zero.

When doctors and therapists teach patients to turn negative thoughts and worries into positive affirmations, the communication process improves and the patient regains self-control and confidence. But there's a problem – the brain does not respond easily to positive words and thoughts, which are no threat to man's survival. The brain does not need to respond as easily as it does to negative thoughts and words.

Analysis: Reaction to positive words in the brain is slower than to negative words or the mind gets attracted more easily towards negative words than positive ones.

Negative thinking is self-perpetuating: The more one engages in negative dialogue, be it at home or at the workplace, the more difficult it becomes to stop. But negative words, spoken with anger, do even greater damage. They send alarm signals to the brain, interfering with the decision-making centers in the frontal lobe and increasing a person's propensity to act rationally.

The story goes that some time ago, a man punished his five-year-old daughter for wasting a roll of expensive gold wrapping paper. Money was tight and he became even more upset when the child pasted the gold paper to decorate a box to put under the Christmas tree.

Nevertheless, the little girl brought the gift box to her father the next morning and said, "This is for you, Daddy." The father was embarrassed at his earlier over-reaction, but his anger flared again when he found the box was empty. He spoke to her in a harsh manner, "Don't you know, young lady, when you give someone a present, there's supposed to be something inside the package?"

The little girl looked up at him with tears in her eyes and said, "Daddy, it's not empty. I blew kisses into it until it was full." The father was humiliated. He fell on his knees and put his arms around his little girl, begging her to forgive him for his undue anger.

An accident took the life of the child only a short time later and it is said that the father kept that gold box by his bed throughout the remaining years of his life.

And whenever he was discouraged or faced a difficult problem, he would open the box and take out an imaginary kiss and remember the love of the child who had put it there.

In a real sense, each of us human being has been given a golden box filled with unconditional love and kisses from our children, family, and friends. There is no other more precious a possession that one can get.

Negative connotations have a longer impact and influence a mind easily than positive ones. Earlier in India, a television company started a brand campaign based on this element, using a demonised figure with the tag line: *'Neighbour's envy, Owner's Pride'.*

This advertisement attracted a lot of attention from the masses and as a part of marketing strategy, it deliberately targeted the sub-conscious psyche of negativity having a longer impact and influence.

Nuggets

- Negative thoughts create a vicious circle and leave you drained.
- Natural tendency is to respond to negative thoughts – Avoid it

"Good thoughts bear good fruit, bad thoughts bear bad fruit – and man is his own gardener."

—James Allen

Notes

(I am being Positive)

Pen down your thoughts/experiences –

Takeaway –

Negative Thoughts Cause Mental Corrosion

Negative Quotient

Let us first go through a sample list of negative indicators that may lead to negative behaviour.

Rate yourself on the following attributes in a scale of 1 to 10:

Sl. No.	Indicators	Rate out of scale of 10
1.	You often use 'cannot do' or 'not possible' or some such words	
2.	You get easily stressed out while encountering problems	
3.	It is easier to control your associates by highlighting their weaknesses	
4.	You feel disappointed when stressed	
5.	You find things difficult to prioritise when they get accumulated	
6.	The first thought that comes to your mind when a severe problem crops up is to find an escape route	

Sl. No.	Indicators	Rate out of scale of 10
7.	You often feel burdened while serving others	
8.	You are argumentative to the point of considering yourself right while the others are wrong	
9.	You often hesitate in exploring alternate/ new solutions for fear of failure	
10.	You get easily tensed over trivial issues	
11.	You find it difficult to appreciate others	
12.	You get impatient if the task is not completed and have the tendency to leave the job unfinished	
13.	You are fearful of taking decisions	
14.	You do not want to take on an unexpected responsibility	
15.	You get disappointed when things don't work according to you	

Calculate your score:

A. Total marks 150

B. Your marks (out of 150) ___

C. Negative Quotient (NQ) (B/A)*100 ___

Negativity is a manifestation of mental corrosion being discussed below:

Mental Corrosion

Corrosion is a menace to society due to the damages and failures of metallic structures and components. It is a sign of the degradation of material properties due to interactions with the environment. While primarily associated with metallic materials, all material types are susceptible to degradation. Like death and taxes, corrosion is something we hope to avoid. Since corrosion of most metals (and many materials for that matter) is inevitable, it is something that we must learn to expect and deal with.

The inevitability of corrosion is due to the spontaneous nature of electrochemical reaction that drives and sustains it. Corrosion is the oxidation of metals. This means that oxygen combines with the metal and forms a new layer. This layer can be good or bad. By far the most important form of corrosion is the rusting of iron.

Rusting is a process of oxidation in which iron combines with water and oxygen to form rust, the reddish-brown crust that forms on the surface of the iron. Because iron is so widely used, e.g. in building construction and in tools, its protection against rusting is important. Rusting can be prevented by excluding air and water from the iron surface by painting, oiling, or greasing, or by plating the iron with a protective coating of another metal. Many alloys of iron are resistant to corrosion. Stainless steel is an alloy of iron with metals like chromium and nickel, which do not corrode because the added metals help form a hard, adherent oxide coating that resists further attack.

Although metals like aluminum, chromium, and zinc corrode more readily than iron, their oxides form a coating that protects the metal from further attack. Rust is brittle and flakes off the surface of iron, continually exposing a fresh surface. Thus, these metals might be a better choice for a product that is liable to rust due to water and air.

The serious consequences of the corrosion process have become a problem of immense worry. In addition to our everyday encounters with this form of degradation, corrosion causes plant shutdowns, wastage of valuable resources, loss or contamination of the product, reduction in efficiency, costly maintenance and expensive conservation. It can also jeopardize the safety and inhibit technological progress.

Just as we understand the mechanism of corrosion of metals and endeavor to control and manage it, corrosion of the human mind due to a variety of corrosive agents can occur. Corrosion of the human mind has a direct impact on the efficiency of the mind. While metallic corrosion weakens the structures and leads them to fail, mental corrosion weakens the mind and damages the character of the human being.

In steel pipeline corrosion, carbon dioxide, sulphur, and moisture play the main role. As per my understanding, it is the combination of moisture with carbon dioxide and sulphur that causes corrosion, including **microbiological-induced corrosion (MIC).** Similar to carbon dioxide and sulphur, negative thoughts and water can be termed as fear and stress. When inner fear and stress blend with negative thoughts, mental corrosion starts and if the negative thoughts are kept inside for long, the mind gets corroded, leading to MIC, which restricts the flow of positive thoughts.

MIC is corrosion which is primarily caused by the bacteria residing in the uneven area inside steel pipelines, wherein it is difficult to flush out the moisture and gradually corrosion colonies form. It is analogous to the negative thoughts which reside and corrode the mind.

Just as corrosive agents like moisture, chlorides, carbon dioxide, hydrogen sulphide combine to attack metals, emotions like stress, fear, and negative thoughts combine to attack the mind and start the deterioration process. Once the mental corrosion starts, negative thoughts dominate the mind, corroding not only the mind but also becoming corrosive since this impacts the minds of other people around.

Like MIC, negative thoughts amplify the influence of anxiety and stress, adding to the woes of a person. We, therefore, need to guard against any ingress of negative thoughts. The antidote for this is to replace these negative thoughts with positive ones through concerted effort to form a protective barrier to preserve the inner core of goodness and give rise to positive energy that has the potential to convert failures into successes; the fear of unknown and converting belief in 'can't' syndrome into 'can do' approach.

So we need to protect our mind against microbiological corrosion to get rid of mental corrosion.

Nuggets

- Identify your negative indicators
- Fear, Stress and negative thoughts render one's mind corroded and useless

"Men are like steel. When they lose their temper, they lose their worth."

—Chuck Norris

Notes

(I am being Positive)

Pen down your thoughts/experiences –

Takeaway –

Are You a Positive or Negative Thinker?

Are You a Positive or Negative Thinker? Learn and Change Your Mode of Thinking

"A man is but the product of his thoughts. What he thinks, he becomes."

—Mahatma Gandhi

The above quote by the great Indian leader under whom India secured freedom summarises his struggle for independence. It is true that one becomes and behaves as per his thoughts. He himself resorted to it in the freedom struggle and gave us the nectar of his experience.

"Positive thinking will let you do everything better than negative thinking will."

—Zig Ziglar (personality development guru)

Positive and negative thoughts can become self-fulfilling prophecies: What we expect can often come true.

If we start off by thinking that we will mess up a task, the chances are that we would. We may not try hard enough to succeed, we will not attract support from other people and we may not perceive the results to be good enough. Thinking positive, on the other hand, is often associated with positive actions and outcomes. We get drawn to and focus on the positive aspects of a situation. We have hope and faith in ourselves and others and work and invest hard to prove that our optimism is warranted. We can enthuse others and they may well 'pitch in' to help us. This makes constructive outcomes to result. At the super positive level, we are able to transform the impossible to possible.

The above two are powerful quotes and if combined, they tell us that if we think positively, we're likely to enjoy positive results. Negative thinking, on the other hand, can lead to outcomes we do not want.

Further, positive, optimistic people are happier and healthier and enjoy more success than those who think negatively. The key difference between them is how they think and interpret the events in their life.

Abraham Lincoln once said, ***'Most folks are about as happy as they want to be.'*** Was he implying that, when it comes to our happiness, we actually have a choice? Apparently, yes. Research abounds on the impact of positive and negative thinking on us and others and the fact that we have the potential to transform ourselves by changing our mind.

The Power of 'Yes'

To overcome the neural bias for negativity, we must repetitively and consciously generate as many positive thoughts as we can. Barbara Fredrickson, one of the founders of Positive

Psychology, discovered that we need to produce at least three positive thoughts and feelings for each expression of negativity. If we express fewer than three, personal and business relationships are likely to fail. This finding correlates with Marcial Losada's research with corporate teams and John Gottman's research with married couples.

Fredrickson, Losada, and Gottman realised that if we want our business and personal relationships to flourish, we need to generate at least five positive messages for each negative utterance we make; for example, 'I'm disappointed' or 'That's not what I had hoped for' are expressions of negativity, as does a facial frown or nod of the head.

Analysis: More positive power is required to overcome the intensity of negative thoughts.

It doesn't even matter if our positive thoughts are irrational; they'll still enhance our sense of happiness, well-being, and satisfaction. In fact, Thinking Positive can help one to build a better and more optimistic attitude towards life. Positive words and thoughts propel the motivational centers of the brain into action and help us build resilience when faced with life's problems.

According to Sonja Lyubomirsky, one of the world's leading researchers on happiness, if we want to develop lifelong satisfaction, we should regularly engage in positive thinking about ourself, share our happiest events with others and savor every positive experience in life.

A piece of advice: Choose your words wisely and speak slowly. This will allow you to interrupt the brain's propensity to become negative and as recent research has shown, the mere repetition of positive words like love, peace, and compassion will turn on specific genes that lower your physical and emotional stress. You'll feel better, live longer and build deeper and more trusting relationships with others, both at home and at the workplace.

As Fredrickson and Losada point out,when we generate a minimum of five positive thoughts to each negative one, we experience *'an optimal range of human functioning'.* That is the power of 'yes'.

Negativity Makes One Try Harder

Let's read the story of a fresh management graduate who tries his hand at entrepreneurship immediately after completing his education.

After returning from Stanford University, having completed my management degree, I was looking at various business opportunities across e-commerce, digital lending, transportation, and others. But one thing that I consistently got as feedback from bankers and prospective investors was that there was no way for two Stanford graduates to be able to crack an online first lending business in India.

The usual sense that we got was them going like 'Tumse Nahi Ho Payega' *(you would not be able to do it). I was also told that the MSME sector is a traditional sector which conducts most of its business offline, hence collecting data from these entities for an online-only lending model was a considerable challenge.*

Such negativity made me take up this business more as a challenge to prove others wrong and I knew that if there was universal skepticism, then the prize to prove everyone wrong would be really great.

Thereby not only did I enter into a lending business but kept it entirely online. Further, even within lending, I chose to join the MSME space though consumer-lending looked easier. Within the lending business also I could have gone for a marketplace or a lead generation model, but then I entered into balance sheet lending.

Even within the SME, in spite of having a better model to underwrite loans in the range of Rs 10 to Rs 30 lakh, I chose to target the Rs 1 lakh loans for Kirana *(provision) shops, which was even more difficult to underwrite.*

So today, if I can count Ribbit Capital, which is one of the most prominent Fintech investors globally, as one of the shareholders of the company, I believe it is mainly due to the fact that as a motto of the company I have always said that we should pick marked dislocations that are deep and hard because if we can crack those, then we have a tremendous head start against the competition.

Thus, Negatives have hidden positives in terms of learning, which could be used if applied to the conversion of failures into success.

Nuggets

- Negative or positive situations are one's own perceptions
- More positive power is required to overcome the intensity of negative thoughts.
- Use hidden positives in negatives to succeed

"There is nothing either good or bad, but thinking makes it so."

—Shakespeare in Hamlet

□

Notes

(I am being Positive)

Pen down your thoughts/experiences –

Takeaway –

3

Positivity

"Success is the outcome of your efforts towards the goal. Continuously train your mind to put your energy in the direction of purpose, including optimism to get it."

—Dr. Ashutosh Karnatak

Doctrine of Positivity

Doctrine of Positivity

Doctrine (from Latin: *doctrine,* meaning 'teaching', 'instruction' or 'doctrine') is a codification of beliefs or a body of teachings or instructions, taught principles or positions, as the essence of lessons in a given branch of knowledge or in a belief system.

The doctrine may also refer to a *principle or law,* in the common-law tradition established through a history of past decisions. Some organisations simply define a *doctrine* as 'that which is taught', or the basis for institutional teaching to its personnel on internal ways of operating.

Based on the above definitions and experience, the doctrine of positivity developed is as below:

Man is Born Positive

By birth, a human being is not negative. Our first impulse is to cooperate. People are born good and are instinctively concerned with the welfare of others. However, upbringing, circumstances, eco-system develop negativity, impacting the mind. It is better to be vigilant and not allow these extraneous factors to hijack the brain.

Push-Pull Theory of Thoughts

Positive thoughts push the person to move ahead while negative thoughts push him back on account of perceived barriers or obstructions, fear or risk. Negative thoughts have more potential than the positive ones. So, in order to move forward, the potential to push power becomes more when the attributes are blended with positivity.

Positivity is DNA of Attributes

A person is born with tremendous potential. Generally, the potential lies dormant along with all the characteristics, like courage, determination, perseverance, etc. The need is to utilise the potential for productive use. Positivity is the DNA of all the attributes. It gives strength to the attributes to release their maximum potential. As per the maturity index of positivity, these attributes gain potency.

Think of Possibilities and Look for Options and Solutions

Positivity enhances mental capability and leads one to think in terms of possibilities, options, and solutions. Positive minds think about the possibilities and options amidst risks and barriers. Positive thoughts are like manure to the mind, which needs to be continuously nourished in order to bear saplings of healthy thoughts and ideas.

Positivity is Infectious

> ***"Attitude is greatly shaped by influence and association."***
>
> —*Jim Rohan*

Positivity is infectious; if one person in a group starts thinking about the solution to a problem, others' minds also start working in that direction. Further, even a person, who never applied the brain to find the answer, starts searching a solution when barriers are encountered.

Positivity Enhances the Capability to see Brighter Side

Positivity is a typical syndrome of transformation. When transformed, one sees strength in self and in associates. This was not visible earlier as one chose to dwell on the weakness of self and others, blaming others for own failures. The person starts to appreciate others and looks on the brighter side of every issue, despite knowing the negative aspect of the same.

Positivity Leads to 'Yes, I can'

Positivity leads to transforming a disability to ability and ability to win-ability. It has got the potential to transform one from 'cannot do' to 'can do'.

Gandhiji's Formula for Positivity

'Think positive, Listen positive, Speak positive.'

Positivity is not only a concept but a phenomenon worthy of adoption. Gandhi, known as the Father of Nation, used three monkeys to convey *'not to hear, think and speak'* anything wrong.

A brief story about three monkeys is as under:

Professor Archer Taylor (1890-1973), a folklorist, writes about a Roman proverb, tracing its origin to a sermon in Paris about AD 1300 and to Gesta Romanorum, *a Latin collection of folklore and legends of the late 14th century.*'Audi, vide, tace, sivisvivere in peace.'*'Hear, see, be silent, if you want to live in peace.'*

It is said that Mahatma Gandhi had very few possessions – a pair of spectacles, sandals, a pocket-watch, a small bowl and plate, and interestingly, the fifth possession was a curio piece of Three Wise Monkeys. The three monkeys find mention in the writings of Confucius, Taoism, and Japanese Shintoism.

In Japanese Shintoism, the three monkeys are:

- Mizaru, who sees no evil
- Kikazaru, who hears no evil and
- Iwazaru, who speaks no evil

These monkeys signify our actions or observations, hearing and speaking. What we do (speak, listen, see) is a function of how we think and what we feel. So the job of these two monkeys was to make the task of Mizaru, Kikazaru and Iwazaru effortless, natural and authentic – what we think, feel and act.

With respect to a positive approach, an analogous model of Gandhi's three monkeys would be:

'Think positive, listen positive, speak positive.'

These factors contribute a lot to information on the approach of an individual.

Think positive: When told to think positive, the subconscious mind receives a signal from a conscious thought on a continuous basis and the formatting of the brain gets done on an ongoing basis. In case of any negative bug in the mind, the conscious mind does the correction by putting patches as done in software.

Listen positive: Listening is an art and is more intense than hearing. It is one of the causes of the communication gap between individuals.

1. Hearing is receiving sound waves through the ears while listening means hearing and understanding what is heard.
2. Hearing is part of the five senses, while listening is the choice to hear and analyse what is heard.
3. Hearing means using your ears only, while listening signifies using the body's other senses too.
4. Listening is observing others' behavior that can add meaning to the message, while hearing merely means receiving sound vibrations.

So from the above, it is clear that listening is more effective than hearing. Listening has a direct impact on the mind as the sensory organ is connected with the brain. Thus it is all the more essential to have a filter before any signal is received by the mind by listening positive. It is again part of the approach of the individual. It is not that negative information signals are also being accepted, but at our level, they need to be filtered and the gathered positive information be sent to the subconscious mind.

Speak positive: The earlier aspects 'think positive and listen positive' are emotional issues; however, speaking positive is the external aspect, by which one gets connected with the environment. From morning to night, one needs to talk to many people in the outer world but also to one's inner self. In order to make a complete internal and external cycle, one is required to speak positive as your word make a difference to others. As it is said, words have power, and if you wish to say 'yes' or 'no' to success or failure, check your inner feelings and also of the person with whom you are communicating.

One day my boss told me, "You say 'yes' to everyone. You should tell explicitly if you shall be able to meet the target or not." I replied smilingly, "When I make a commitment to someone, I internally calculate the time line based on my experience, situation, and resources. Although I may be a bit optimistic, I am by and large successful in meeting the target. It is, in fact, a commitment to the self, which inspires me to accomplish the objective." Also, it challenges the teammates to work towards the target dates. So it is better to speak positive as it conveys positive vibes in others' minds.

Thus, in order to develop a positive approach, Gandhiji's formula, '*Think positive, Listen positive, Speak positive' should be imbibed.*

"One kind word can warm three winter months."

—Japanese proverb

Notes

(I am being Positive)

Pen down your thoughts/experiences –

Takeaway –

"'Defeat' itself get defeated when you have Everest like determination to reach the goal."

—Dr. Ashutosh Karnatak

Hanuman Syndrome

Swami Vivekananda would often echo what the *Upanishads* have declared: '*Arise, awake and stop not till you reach your goal.*' The tendency to rest and take breaks during work is a major obstacle to success. *Rishis* and sages have advised us that once we set out to achieve something, we should not stop until we succeed. Swami Chinmayananda would say, 'If we rest, we rust'.

In Goswami Tulsidas's *Shri Ramcharitmanas*, Hanuman's eagerness to serve Shri Rama, coupled with his sincere efforts, helped him cross all obstacles of temptation and move forward on the path of success.

Hanuman was blessed with tremendous power. All that was required was to make him realise his dormant power. Similarly, internal power/energy needs to be discovered within because each of us has tremendous power lying dormant within us.

Hanuman encountered three obstacles while flying over the 800-mile ocean stretch to reach Lanka in search of Sita. First appeared Mainak Parvat, a pleasure resort in the middle of the ocean. Hanuman was invited to rest for a while, but he replied, "Until I have completed Rama's work, there is no rest for me."

Hanuman had full faith in the Lord and he jumped across the ocean. Whenever our work is noble, we should not hesitate to pursue it to completion. Even when we start with enthusiasm, there is a temptation to rest or take a break and enjoy some wayside distraction. Once we give in to it, the law of inertia takes over and prevents us from moving ahead.

Viveka and *chaturtha* – wisdom to discriminate and the alertness to judge situations and act accordingly – are the qualities required to progress towards success. Noble virtues are also necessary.

As Hanuman continued to fly across the ocean, there came Sursa, the mother of snakes. She obstructed his path and threatened to swallow him. Hanuman pleaded with her to let him go and promised that on completing the Lord's work, he would return and readily enter her mouth. But, she showed no compassion. So, Hanuman increased himself in size and Sursa opened her mouth wide, but Hanuman became larger still. Then, Hanuman instantly became small, went into her large open mouth and came out before she could close it. He said, "I entered your mouth and you did not swallow me, so now you must let me go." Sursa was pleased with Hanuman's intelligence and wished him a successful journey.

We must know when to use force and when not to use. At the same time, we should not make anything a prestige issue. Often, when we insist on asserting our opinion, we lose sight of the objective and do not move towards it. The goal is important; we must know when to act big and when to act small, when to be humble and when to be strong.

As he proceeded on his journey, Hanuman felt he was being pulled down into the waters by a mysterious force. It was the demon Sinika, who, having dragged her victims down, planned to devour them. Sinika stands for jealousy, which can never bear the rise of another person. It is jealousy that pulls us down and devours us. Jealousy in one's heart and jealousy invoked in the hearts of others is the cause of downfall.

One should not encourage jealousy and other such negative, self-degrading tendencies to develop in one's heart. They should be destroyed immediately, just as Hanuman mercilessly killed Sinika with one blow.

Nuggets

- Positivity is innate
- Awaken the Hanuman within and realise your dormant powers
- Ignore all evil and focus on ***Think positive, listen positive, speak positive***
- Positive person inspires others also to excel

"It is the nature of man to rise to greatness if greatness is expected of him."

—John Steinbeck, author

Notes

(I am being Positive)

Pen down your thoughts/experiences –

Takeaway –

Mental Positivism

Your all actions are the manifestation of your thoughts, which are the reactions of neurotransmitters in the brain. Be an architect of your mind, develop pen space to reside positive and inspirational ideas also have windows to take out negative ones.

Mental Positivism

A successful person is one who bounces back faster than others in case of any failure. This phenomenon of bouncing back is related to mental positivism. A mentally positive person can bounce back faster than a negative-attitude person.

In scientific terms, it can be co-related to the concept of magnetism, under which most materials can be classified as diamagnetic, paramagnetic or ferromagnetic.

Diamagnetic materials have a weak, negative susceptibility to magnetic fields. They are slightly repelled by a magnetic field and the material does not retain the magnetic properties when the external field is removed.

Paramagnetic materials have a small positive susceptibility to magnetic fields. These materials are slightly attracted by a magnetic field and the material does not retain the magnetic properties when the external field is removed.

Ferromagnetic materials have a large positive susceptibility to an external magnetic field. They exhibit a strong attraction to magnetic fields and are able to retain their magnetic properties even after the external field has been removed.

Material	Magnetic Property	Metal Property
Dia	Nil	No impact of positive forces on a closed mind.
Para	Moderate till external impact is present	Becomes positive when the positive forces are present, but need frequent charging.
Ferro	Permanent	Remain perpetually positive, irrespective of a positive field.

In *Mahabharata*, Arjun was in the midst of the battlefield where Lord Krishna was motivating him to fight. He was in dia-positivism mode. Krishna was the positive magnetic field. Arjun was finding it difficult but the positivity of Krishna overcame his negative mental state. After a lot of persuasion and arguments between him and Lord Krishna, his mental frame became ferro-positive and the rest is history. Think about a situation where the mental state of Arjun could not have changed.

In order to fight the battle of life, positivity is required. People with a negative mindset have already lost the battle before it has even started.

It is necessary to have the baseline data about self-positivity. What is your positivity index and which type of person you are can be assessed by answering the following questionnaire (Be truthful to yourself while answering:

Positivity Quotient: Rate yourself on the following attributes in a scale of 1 to 10:

Sl. No.	Attribute	Rating Out of 10
1	Are you generally smiling	
2	Do you remain unruffled when problems arise	
3	Do you have a generally helpful attitude	
4	Are you optimistic and always see a silver lining to every cloud	
5	Do you see a half glass filled or half glass empty	
6	Do you look at strengths than weaknesses of associates	
7	Do you generally act without prejudice	
8	Are you fearless	
9	Do you take decisions	
10	Do you generally look for a solution	
11	Do you extend help to others	
12	Are you generally happy	
13	In case of obstacles and challenges, what is the level of your excitement	
14	Do you like challenges	
15	Do you appreciate others for their goodness or good deeds	
16	Do you inspire others	
17	Do you manage your time well	
18	Do you bounce back after any failure	
19	Are you open-minded on controversial issues	
20	Are you open to suggestions for improvement in your work and willing to go an extra mile to handle extra work	
21	Do you handle stress well	

Calculate your score:

A. Total marks 210

B. Your marks (out of 210) ___

C. Positive Quotient (PQ) (B/A)*100 ___

If the Positivity Quotient (PQ)% score is less than 75, you require a change of mental software.

Positive Psychology*

As defined by the Positive Psychology Center at the University of Pennsylvania, "**Positive Psychology**" is the scientific study of the strengths and virtues that enable individuals and communities to thrive. The field is founded on the belief that people want to lead meaningful and fulfilling lives, to cultivate what is best within themselves, and to enhance their experiences of love, work, and play.

Positive Psychology, though seemingly easy to understand, has certain specific aspects to it, which need to be understood for appropriately practicing it. Another definition says Positive psychology is a science of positive aspects of human life, such as happiness, well-being and flourishing. It can be summarised in the words of its founder, **Martin Seligman, as the 'scientific study of optimal human functioning that aims to discover and promote the factors that allow individuals and communities to thrive'.**

Psychology has more often than not emphasised the shortcomings of individuals as compared with their potential. But Positive Psychology is based on an approach that focuses on the potential. It is not targeted at fixing problems, but is focused on researching things that make life worth living instead. **It aims to bring someone out of their negative zone and build on the positivity.**

---

* *Source – Literature survey: To give an idea to readers on positive psychology*

In short, positive psychology is concerned not with how to improve a -10 score to -2 score but focuses on getting someone out of the negative zone and transform and build upon one's positive score or alternatively transform one's score of +3 to +10, an enormous addition to one's potential.

The aim is to start at Positive (1P) and move on to 2P, 3P and so on. The focus is on the building blocks of positivity and creating a strong and well designed building – in the human context, it means building a strong and well groomed and positive personality.

According to the research undertaken in this field, this orientation in psychology was established about ten years ago and it is a rapidly developing field. Its aspiration is to bring solid empirical research into areas such as well-being, flow, personal strengths, wisdom, creativity, psychological health and characteristics of positive groups and institutions.

Three levels of positive psychology

The science of positive psychology operates on three different levels - the subjective level, the individual level and the group level.

The subjective level includes the study of positive experiences such as joy, well-being, satisfaction, contentment, happiness, optimism and flow. This level is about feeling good, rather than doing good or being a good person.

At the next level, the aim is to identify the constituents of the 'good life' and the personal qualities that are necessary for being a 'good person', through studying human strengths and virtues, future-mindedness, capacity for love, courage, perseverance, forgiveness, originality, wisdom, interpersonal skills and giftedness.

Finally, at the group or community level, the emphasis is on civic virtues, social responsibilities, altruism, civility, tolerance, work ethics, positive institutions and other factors that contribute to the development of citizenship and communities.

This takes us back to our original premise – "Though Positive Psychology seems to be well understood by everyone, there are number of aspects to it". It actually goes through various stages of development of an individual and hence forms an important part of knowing oneself. The growth goes through the development of one's intelligence – and moving towards higher levels of Emotional Quotient. The combination of IQ and EQ, when supported by Positive action, helps one develop the Positivity Quotient (PQ).

Positive psychology – Moving into the Positive Side of human mind

Psychology as a subject has indeed gone through different phases. According to positive psychologists, for most of its life mainstream psychology (sometimes also referred to as 'psychology as usual') has been concerned with the negative aspects of human life. There have been pockets of interest in topics such as creativity, optimism and wisdom, but these have not been united by any grand theory or a broad, overarching framework. This rather negative state of affairs was not the original intention of the first psychologists, but came about through a historical accident.

Prior to the Second World War, psychology had three tasks, which were to: cure mental illness, improve normal lives and identify and nurture high talent. However, after the war, the last two tasks somehow got lost, leaving the field to concentrate predominantly on the first one. How did that happen? Given that psychology as a science depends heavily on the funding of governmental bodies, it is not hard to guess what happened to the resources after World War II. Understandably, facing a human crisis on such an enormous scale, all available resources were poured into learning about and the treatment of psychological illness and psychopathology.

The failure to address the improvement of normal lives and the identification and to nurture high talent was realised in later years. Just to illustrate, if you were to say to your friends that you were going to see a psychologist, what is the most likely response that you would get? ‘What’s wrong with you?’. How likely are you to hear something along the lines of: ‘Great! Are you planning to concentrate on self-improvement?’.

Many psychologists admit that we have little knowledge of what makes life worth living or of how normal people flourish under usual, rather than extreme, conditions. The Western world has long overgrown the rationale for an exclusively disease model of psychology.

Perhaps now is the time to re-address the balance by using psychology resources to learn about normal and flourishing lives, rather than lives that are in need of help. Perhaps now is the time to gather knowledge about strengths and talents, high achievement (in every sense of this word), the best ways and means of self-improvement, fulfilling work and relationships, and a great art of ordinary living carried out in every corner of the planet. This is the rationale behind the creation of positive psychology.

However, positive psychology is still nothing else but psychology, adopting the same scientific method. It simply studies different (and often far more interesting) topics and asks slightly different questions, such as ‘what works?’ rather than ‘what doesn’t?’ or ‘what is right with this person?’ rather than ‘what is wrong?’

Scientific Aspects of Positivity

Hormones

It is indeed a fact that secretion of hormones from various glands controls our life. When hormones, such as non-adrenaline are over- or under-produced, the emotional state can become imbalanced either negatively or positively. Thoughts, bad or good, act on the brain to release neurotransmitters that affect the mood or health and physical responses in the body. ***Neuro-transmitters which enhance attention and pleasure are named as dopamines and those which reduce fear and worry are known as serotonins.*** If someone is under stress, his or her heart starts beating fast and the body releases these powerful stress hormones – epinephrine, cortisol, and adrenalin. When these hormones are secreted continuously, they affect the body, inducing brain aging, increase in fat, muscle and bone loss. On the contrary, in the case of Thinking Positive or avoidance of negative words, use of positive words checks the secretion of negative hormones and facilitates improvement in health.

Read the below story:

As I sat in the park after my morning walk, My wife came and slumped next to me.

She had completed her 30-minute jog. We chatted for a while. She said she is not happy in life. I looked up at her sheer disbelief since she seemed to have the best of everything in life.

"Why do you think so?"

"I don't know. Everyone tells I have everything needed, but I am not happy.

"Then I questioned myself, am I happy? "No," was my inner voice reply.

Now, that was an eye-opener for me.

I began my quest to understand the real cause of my unhappiness.

I couldn't find one.

I dug deeper, read articles, spoke to life coaches but nothing made sense.

At last my doctor friend gave me the answer which put all my questions and doubts to rest.

I implemented those and will say I am a lot happier person.

She said, there are four hormones which determine a human's happiness -

1. **Endorphins,**
2. **Dopamine,**
3. **Serotonin, and**
4. **Oxytocin.**

It is important we understand these hormones,as we need all four of them to stay happy.

Let's look at the first hormone, the Endorphins.

When we exercise, the body releases Endorphins. This hormone helps the body cope with the pain of exercising. We then enjoy exercising because these Endorphins will make us happy. Laughter is another good way of generating Endorphins.

We need to spend 30 minutes exercising every day, read or watch funny stuff to get our day's dose of Endorphins.

The second hormone is Dopamine.

In our journey of life, we accomplish many little and big tasks, it releases various levels of Dopamine.

When we get appreciated for our work at the office or at home, we feel accomplished and good, that is because it releases Dopamine.

This also explains why most housewives are unhappy since they rarely get acknowledged or appreciated for their work. Once, we join work, we buy a car, a house, the latest gadgets, a new house so forth. In each instance, it releases Dopamine and we become happy.

Now, do we realise why we become happy when we shop?

The third hormone Serotonin is released when we act in a way that benefits others.

When we transcend ourselves and give back to others or to nature or to the society, it releases Serotonin. Even,providing useful information on the internet like writing information blogs, answering peoples questions on Quora or Facebook groups will generate Serotonin.

That is because we will use our precious time to help other people via our answers or articles.

The final hormone is Oxytocin, is released when we become close to other human beings.

When we hug our friends or family Oxytocin is released. The 'Jadoo Ki Jhappi' from Munnabhai does really work. Similarly, when we shake hands or put our arms around someone's shoulders, various amounts of Oxytocin is released.

So, it is simple, we have to exercise every day to get **Endorphins,**

We have to accomplish little goals and get **Dopamine,**

We need to be nice to others to get **Serotonin** and

Finally hug our kids,friends, and families to get **Oxytocin** and we will be happy.

When we are happy, we can deal with our challenges and problems better.

Now, we can understand *why we need to hug a child who has a bad mood.*

So to.

Make your child more and more happy day by day ...

1. **Motivate him to play on the ground-Endorphins**
2. **Appreciate your child for his small big achievements-Dopamine**
3. **Inculcate sharing habit through you to your child - Serotonin**
4. **Hug your child-Oxytocin**

Role of Mind

Our attitudes and actions are functions of our mind, which is the nucleus of every living being. Therefore, it is better to understand the mind first. For a common person, our mind is situated inside our scalp which, though small in size, does all the big works, like research, manufacturing, service, etc.

Every action flows from the mind which primarily has two parts: an active or conscious mind and a passive or subconscious mind.

An active mind is that portion of the mind which plays a role in day-to-day actions, whereas the subconscious mind helps in shaping our thinking pattern. An active mind receives signals from the subconscious mind before taking any action. Thus the subconscious mind needs to be understood in detail. We are born with stored memories of our past births located in the subconscious mind, which are generally stored as a heap of paper. Our need is to format the subconscious mind. Sometimes we are unable to recall the name of any person or forget the answer to a question during the examinations or see dreams of different types, encounter unknown fears, prejudices, and negative thinking /attitude. All this is due to the subconscious mind.

Pollyanna Principle

Pollyanna is a 1913 novel by the American author, Eleanor H. Porter and is considered a classic in children's literature. The book's success led Porter to pen down the sequel – *Pollyanna Grows Up* (1915). Eleven more *Pollyanna* sequels, known as *Glad Books*, were later published with most of them written by Elisabeth Borton or Harriet Lummis Smith.

Due to the book's fame, *Pollyanna* became a byword for someone who, like the protagonist, has an unfailingly optimistic outlook – *a subconscious bias towards positivity is often described as the Pollyanna principle.*

The Pollyanna principle (also called Pollyannaism or positivity bias) is the tendency among people to remember pleasant incidents more vividly than unpleasant ones. Research on the subject indicates that at the subconscious level, the mind has a tendency to focus on the happy moments, while at the conscious level, the tendency is to focus on the negative.

According to the Pollyanna principle, the brain processes information that is pleasing and agreeable in a more precise and exact manner as compared to unpleasant information. We actually tend to remember our past experiences as brighter than they actually were. People respond easily to positive stimuli and avoid negative stimuli, taking longer to recall what is unpleasant or threatening than what is pleasant and safe. They report that they encounter positive stimuli more frequently than they actually do.

However, the Pollyanna principle does not always apply to individuals suffering from depression or anxiety or those who tend to either have more depressive realism or negative bias.

Further, in 1962, Rogger Sperry won the Nobel Prize for identifying two hemispheres of the brain that are responsible for separate intellectual functions, based on a scientific analysis using Magnetic Resonance Imaging (MRI) of the brain/mind. It was established that the mind has two hemispheres, right and left, whose brief roles are as under:

Left Hemisphere	Right Hemisphere
Right Side of the Body	**Left Side of the Body**
Mathematics	Creative
Verbal	Artistic
Logical	Visual
Facts	Intuition
Deductions	Ideas
Analysis	Imagination
Words of a song	Tune of a song
Finer details	Multiprocessing/Multitasking

The left side of the brain controls the right side of the body whereas the right side of the brain controls the left. It is said that we use only 10 % of our mental capacity. It seems to be correct as most persons do not use their right side of the brain. Therefore, since childhood, people are told to indulge in some artistic pursuits as it helps to develop the left side of the brain, which controls imagination, artistic bent of mind and creative pursuits. ***Development of Positive Thinking is attributed to the right side of the brain, which needs to be used for its development.***

Thus after learning something about the brain, it can be concluded that in order to develop positive thinking, we need to sharpen our subconscious mind and the right hemisphere of the brain.

Scientific Aspects of Thinking Positive

Every person is a bundle of energy which helps in his survival. Generally, the total energy is the sum of external energy and internal energy.

Total energy (TE) = External Energy (EE) + Internal Energy (IE) .

External Energy is basically the energy which develops inside the body due to our diet, intake of nutrients, etc.

Internal energy is broadly the spiritual energy, which one acquires through various exercises like meditation, Vipassana, etc. and other spiritual exercises. But the most important aspect of this is the attitude of the person, which helps him to optimize internal energy.

As per physics,

Power P= VxI

= Vx V/R (I = Current, R= Resistance, V= Voltage)

= V*2/R

Here, *R* is the internal resistance posed by the mind in the form of anger, irritation, frustration, etc. These can be reduced through a positive attitude. In case this *R* gets reduced, the power of internal energy reaches the maximum, leading to maximisation of the total energy of the person.

It has been seen that the external energy can be used to its maximum when the internal energy level is better, i.e. if internal energy is less, the consumption of external energy increases. Thus the power of Thinking Positive is:

P = *(Attitude)*2/* R

Where* R *= internal resistance

It is obvious from the above formula that the power of thinking will be more positive if internal resistance is less. It means that if someone is a positive-thinking person, he can use his mental powers up to optimum limits.

Nuggets

- Embrace magnetic field of positive people around you.
- Use your positive quotient to Influence others
- Explore your right side of brain – the imaginative, artistic bend of mind
- Reduce internal resistance through positivity

The saying goes,

"Change is not the problem; resistance to change is the problem."

□

Notes

(I am being Positive)

Pen down your thoughts/experiences –

Takeaway –

4

Transformation Journey

"We know what we are but not what we may be."

—Ophelia in Hamlet,

by William Shakespeare, 1894'

Positive winning Personality

Life is for success and happiness. Most of the time we accord priority to Success than happiness and continuously strive for it.The aim is to develop a winnable personality,who has developed the habit of winning. Positivity has important role in producing Winnable characters. Positive thinking works as a catalyst to the reaction of different attributes required for success.

"You were born to win, but to be a winner, you must plan to win, prepare to win, and expect to win."

—Zig Ziglar

What you feed to your mind will determine your character, personality and all other things that happen to you in your life. In many books on Positive Personality, the word Mental Diet is used - when you feed your mind with positive affirmations, conversations, information, readings, audio programs, and thoughts, you develop a more positive attitude and personality. Therefore you take more decisive actions and thereby, you exude more positive energy. Over a period of time, you create a bigger circle positive associates and become more influential. You enjoy greater confidence and self-esteem. We have often come across in computer parlance, the word GIGO - Garbage in, Garbage out. Conversely and not surprisingly, GIGO also applies for "Goodies in, Goodies out."

Mental fitness is like physical fitness. You develop high levels of self-esteem and a positive attitude with training and practice.

We present here the 11 keys to developing a positive personality which can result in your transformation – to a confident and affirmative action-oriented character.

Positive Thinking and Visualisation

Any action starts with thinking. Positive responses start with thinking positive. Perhaps the most powerful ability that you have is the ability to think through and visualise and see your goals as already accomplished. Destination or ultimate objective must always be part of your thought process. Create a bright, exciting picture of your target and your ideal life, and replay this picture in your mind over and over.

Napoleon Hill, the famous author, emphasised a great deal on the power of mind, auto-suggestion and visualising success in your mind. All improvement in your life begins with an improvement in your mental pictures. As you "see" yourself on the inside, you will "be" on the outside.

Positive Eco-System

Your surrounding eco-system at home and workplace, where one spends most of the time, has a profound impact in shaping your personality. If one seriously look at it, the choice of people and the environment is often determined by you. The choice of the people with whom you live, work, and an associate will have more of an impact on your emotions and your success than any other factor.

Decide today to associate with winners, with people who focus on professional progress, with positive people, with people who are happy and optimistic and who are going somewhere with their lives. Imagine you are surrounded by such people described above. Your personality will imbibe lots of their qualities while strengthening your own good merits. In marketing, there is something called a primary product with certain core qualities of its own.

Then there is an augmented product, which is enhanced, packaged and presented in a proper, protected and clean manner, in order to be of long term use and which will also attract customers. Similarly, in our professional and personal lives, there are lots of possibilities of augmenting oneself. Right ecosystem and people greatly aid in that process.

Avoid negative people. Avoid gossip mongers. Negative people are the primary source of most of life's unhappiness. Resolve that from today onward; you are not going to have stressful or negative people in your life. Taking out negativism is an essential part of cleansing your environment and thoughts.

"Show me your friends and I would tell you who you are."
Vanilla Ice

"Surround yourself with those who only lift you higher."
Oprah Winfrey

"People inspire you, or they drain you – pick them wisely."
Hans F. Hansen

Positive ideas and content

Body health is decided by the food you take. Just as your body is healthy to the degree to which you eat healthy, nutritious meals, your mind is robust to the degree to which you feed it with "mental nutrients" rather than "mental junk." Read books, magazines, and articles that are educational, inspirational, or motivational. Feed your mind with information and ideas that are uplifting and that make you feel happy and more confident about yourself and your world. Acquire new ideas and knowledge which would help you grow professionally. Such content, rich with new ideas, knowledge and positive messages will help you think and act better and make you more capable and competent in your field. Interact with those who add value to your thought processes, knowledge and personality. This will definitely make you stronger and confident besides adding to your self-worth.

Positive Learning

If one recalls, many of us would have started with limited resources and limited or no money at all. Virtually, all fortunes begin with augmenting oneself with knowledge, ideas, and skills, which one offers to an organisation or at work and earns his resources. All the people who are at the top positions today started at the bottom, and also would have fallen several times during their journey. Each time, they have said, **"Yes, I Can"** and moved on to next higher level. During multiple falls, they have never given up. They have moved on continuously towards the summit, every time saying, **Prayas, Ek Aur Kadam (PEAK)** and no wonder they have reached the PEAK today in their work or profession.

This is beautifully summarised by one of the authors - The miracle of lifelong learning and personal improvement is what takes you from rags to riches, from poverty to affluence, and from under achievement to success and financial independence. Napoleon Hill talks about Monetary Riches as well as Lifetime Riches – which is more holistic. Another author Jim Rohn said, **"Formal education will make you a living, self-education will make you a fortune**.". Continuous learning has no substitute. Successful personalities have learned from their failures and marched on, and they never stopped for a moment to get sucked into the quagmire of past failures.

When you dedicate yourself to learning and growing and becoming better and more effective in your thoughts and actions, you take complete control of your life and dramatically increase the speed at which you move upward to greater heights.

Positive Health Habits

Only when you have the canvas adequately placed, you can create a beautiful painting. Take excellent care of your physical health and wellness. Resolve today that you are going to live to be eighty or ninety years and still have active interactions and quality times with your circle of positive ambassadors. Eat healthy food, natural and nutritious, and eat them sparingly and in proper balance. A nutritional and balanced diet will have an immediate, positive effect on your thoughts and feelings.

Resolve to get regular exercise, at least two hundred minutes of motion per week, to walk, to run, to swim, to bicycle, or to work out on equipment in the gym. When you exercise on a regular basis, you feel happier and healthier and experience lower levels of stress and fatigue than a person who sits on the couch and watch television all evening. Mainly, get ample rest and relaxation. You need to recharge your batteries on a regular basis, especially when you are going through periods of stress or difficulty.

Vince Lombardi once said, "Fatigue makes cowards of us all."

Some of the factors that predispose us to negative emotions of all kinds are poor health habits, sleep deprivation, lack of exercise, and nonstop work. Seek balance in your life and achieve them.

Positive Expectation and Attraction

Law of Attraction is one of the most powerful techniques that one can practice to become a confident and well-rounded person.

This results in positive actions leading to positive outcomes and better results in your life. Your expectations become your own self-fulfilling prophesies. As Napoleon Hill says, whatever you expect, with confidence and self-belief, seems to come into your life. Best things in life are in and around us. We need to prepare our mind to welcome them. Good things would not like to enter your mind as unwelcome guests. They follow the rules of the law of attraction.

Positivity is contagious. In fact, due to circumstances, the human becomes so negative that his mind is covered with many firewalls as a software system have. A software firewall is for anti-spam, but the human mental walls are anti-positive thoughts.

"Expect to achieve great goals and create a wonderful life for yourself. When you constantly expect good things to happen, you will seldom be disappointed".

Positive Actions

Positive Actions are what you ultimately do and perform after acquiring all the positivity traits – all the thoughts and habits acquired from the key aspects of a positive personality described above. Your actions will have a positive impact on all the people around you. You become the source of positivity and conveyor of positivity. Chains of positive responses created around multiple circles of human groups ultimately result in a transformation of an organisation as a whole or a society at large. Such large scale transformation is the primary objective of becoming a positive personality at an individual level. It starts with **"YOU."**

Winning Personality Attributes

HIP (Honesty, Integrity and Positive Attitude) formula

"The greatest pleasure in life is doing what people Say you cannot do"

—Walter Bagehot

Generally, in life, we remember the winner than a loser. Loser gets sympathy; whereas the winner receives laurels from all the corners. In the annals of history,Sikandar is known as a symbol of the winner,and in day to day life, the winners are quoted synonymous to Sikandar. Are winners born winners – No. All human beings are the same at the time of birth, but their attitude in life makes them a winner, which they develop in the course of life by experience or by deliberate practice.

Honesty is the most critical aspect for the winner to practice

Honesty is related to conscience and conscience is similar to the environment, through which we traverse to attaining adulthood. In fact, after reaching adulthood, our attitudes become fixed. **One of the children used to bring a pencil and rubber of his classmate to his home. When the mother checked the bag of a child, she found extra things. After inquiring, the child explained the position and was advised by the mother to return the same next day.** In this case, the mother has sown the seed of honesty in the mind of the child, which was engraved in his mind and led to take him in the path of virtue."

Dr. Mortimer Feinberg, author of Corporate Bigamy, interviewed one hundred top executives with fortune 500 companies. Those men said that anyone who thinks he can get to the top and stay there without honesty is dumb. Thus it is not only to be honest but also to look like honest is more important.

"Adversity is the trial of principle. Without it, a man hardly knows whether he is honest or not."

—Henry Fielding

Integrity is a vital element in building a forceful personality and a fundamental principle of permanent success. Thus our mind must be firmly based on truth. In early day's, people used to give the 'VARDAAN', and once words are provided, they are to be fulfilled at any cost. The example of King Dasrath giving words to Kaikei is well known and how he met the proposed. A winner requires this type of integrity. Integrity gives birth to Credibility. That is why it is told to "Walk the Talk."I have seen that most of the people commit to others but fail to fulfill the promise. It leads to a loss of credibility.

A positive attitude is another most desirable quality for a winning personality. The critical and decisive factor in life is not what happens to us, but the approach we take towards what happens. **Thinking Plus(Positive) is a Winner's Attitude**. You are sure to win if you have a positive attitude. Failure is meant to achieve goals. It is indeed like the sun rising from the east that you set a goal; you get it. There might be hurdles on the way but don't leave it, have a positive thinking every day that you are going to win and you get it.

"If you wish to succeed, you must give your whole mind, heart, and soul to your work.

To do this, you must love your work; in no other way can you be diligent. It is not talents or acquirements, but enthusiasm and energy that win the battle of life.

Resolve to complete anything to its completion. Realise that no weak-hearted, intermittent effort will achieve the desired results. Hold steadily before your mind a single great ideal and purpose and make each day's effort count substantially towards your personal progress.

"Success in life is not for those who run fast, but for those who keep running and always on the move."

—Bangambiki Habyarimana, Pearls of Eternity

Notes

(I am being Positive)

Pen down your thoughts/experiences –

Takeaway –

A step towards Thinking Positive

After going through the attributes leading to winnable positive personality, let us look into some of the pre-requisite which act as catalyst in a step towards Thinking Positive :

- Positive Desire
- Positive Aggression
- Be optimistic
- Positive affirmations

Develop Positive Desire

Desire is the first point to consider before starting any work or assignment. Any job done without desire yields unsatisfactory results and on analysing the same, one finds that desire to the level of fructification of the task to succeed was not present. Recently, I spoke to my son who is in Class X and has to appear for the Board examination, which requires a lot of preparation. As parents, we can provide all the resources like study material, tuitions, nutritious food, guidance, etc., but the action to study has to be taken by him only. I advised him that if the desire to excel is not there, he would not be able to secure good marks. Results are directly proportional to desire, which can be transformed into an ardent desire through the thought that '*it must happen' and the desire has to be developed to achieve something.*'

Life is like a stage where the one who performs is appreciated when the show gets over. Life too has to be dealt in a similar manner. By developing the desire to do something will bring about an overall change in one's attitude, approach, and productivity.

Take the example of the Chinese, who despite belonging to a communist county, possess the desire to spread their consumer products all over the world, ranging from kitchen-knife, calculators, music system, electrical appliances, toys, key chains, etc. at the lowest possible price. Chinese goods have become part of the middle-class Indian household. This would not have been possible if their country's leaders and the people had not desired it to be so. So why do we lag? It is simply because of the lack of ardent desire to produce consumer goods at cheap prices.

Recently, in one of the articles, the father of Bill Gates stated that during childhood, Bill used to slip out of his room in the basement to the nearest café and work on computers. Next morning, Bill would pretend as if he had been inside the house at night. This example shows *how Bill Gates at a very young age had the desire to achieve something. The result of his labor is known to all of us. He has been a normal human being except for possessing the desire to achieve something.*

The growth of Reliance group to what it is today is the result of the desire and hard work of the late Dhirubhai Ambani.

Ravana wanted to possess Sita, so he decided to abduct her. Here the desire was adverse, hence he met a fatal end. The need is to have a positive desire. Let us try to learn some of the methodologies for generating positive desire.

(1) Train the child in childhood itself: Comfort leads to laziness and kills the desire or longing to achieve something. Normally parents try to fulfill every possible requirement of their child and when he finds that the parents are willing to do anything for him, his mental attitude shifts towards laziness, making him sluggish, both physically and mentally.

Hence the prerequisite is to generate the desire to achieve since early childhood itself. It is generally seen that a child from a poor family secures better marks and excels in life than a child from a well-to-do family. In fact, deficiencies give birth to the desire to acquire and reach somewhere and this directs his or her actions.

Thus, inculcate the desire to rise high in life through hard work and perseverance. It may be in music, studies, games, painting, etc. but the earlier it is developed, the better it would be for him. ***Desire can make a person act like a machine.***

(2) The desire to do something for inner satisfaction only; not for the sake of others: The current trend is that if a person conducts his regular duties out of his sense of responsibilities, he desires some advantage. At the professional level, a person who performs his duties up to the mark might be doing so to oblige others. This perception needs to be changed altogether. We have to alter our thinking and convince ourselves that we are performing some action as it would impart internal satisfaction and not merely please others. During childhood, Bill Gates, being nicknamed Trey, used to spend hours at a local company dealing in computers. He used to identify the bugs that would crash them. As mentioned above, he would often sneak out at night. He did maximum work overtime and the reward was the feeling of pleasure. Understand the sublime fact that at this point of childhood itself, the seed to do something in the field of the computer had started germinating.

Therefore, develop a desire that gives internal satisfaction and self-pleasure.

(3) Injection of positive desire: It's a matter of feelings only. When sick, tablets are given for an early recovery from sickness. In the same way, a desireless syndrome or the feeling *that whatever one has is enough for him*. Such a thought is detrimental to his growth.

Have you ever thought of becoming rich or remain healthy or become a poet or an efficient or a good husband or a good boss?

The answer may be partial 'yes' and partially 'no'. At this point, it is advisable to introspect. You may discover that you have never given a thought to this as you did not possess the time or the desire to reach somewhere in life.

From here starts the therapy regimen. Take the injection of positive desire which will direct your mind to develop the desired goal. This becomes the stepping stone to your progress.

(4) Desire management: *You may have the desire to achieve something but you do not know in what field it should be. You may be caught in a dilemma regarding your desire.* The aim here is to emphasise the fact that whatever task you undertake, work towards its completion with desire. Develop a passion for the same so that you may achieve the desired results. Desire the thing which is closest to your heart. Many people do not put their hearts in the task because they do not know what their desire is. Thus there is a need to:

- *Prioritise your desire on a short-term or long-term basis and manage it as per the requirements*
- *Do not leave the task incomplete*

- *Explore the meaning of life.*

Conclusively, it can be said that:

- *One has to develop a desire for any task for its effective completion*
- *The outcome of the work should be for internal satisfaction and pleasure*
- *Learn the art of prioritising the desires*
- *As soon as the level of desire goes down, take the vaccination called positive desire*

Positive Aggression

'Maintain the light of struggle within you; let it not die. It is a force leading you to success.'

There are a few people who are ready to fight with energy and determination to fulfill their desire – it could be the desire to end hunger by fighting against all the odds. Such people are born fighters, not against anybody but against their own weaknesses. They compete against themselves, always trying to outdo what have already achieved. They may be satisfied with what they have, but they are never satisfied with what they are. It goes without saying that there is nowadays cut-throat competition, but they are a cut above the rest.

Not all struggles are bad; some are good enough to take you to a higher level. Like in the steeplechase, runners have to run fast and jump sufficiently high over the obstacles to win; similarly one has to overcome the impediments that the life throws to test one's mettle. It is the faint-hearted who leave the race halfway, feeling depressed and deflated.

Once an astrologer saw the palm of a person and forecast that the latter might face tension in the near future. To the astrologer's surprise, the person felt good. He said, "I need tension to go ahead. It leads me to progress. If these are not there, then my mental faculties refuse to work and develop." This answer clearly describes the need for the struggle inside you. Struggle, though a negative word, offers positive rewards, like success, confidence, self-esteem and so on. A man without a struggle seldom achieves his goal in life. History is replete with names like Mahatma Gandhi, Abraham Lincoln, Nelson Mandela, who at some stage or other faced all kinds of adversities in life. But they never gave up their fight because the fire in the belly kept on burning and rekindling it if it started growing weak.

An optimum level of struggle is required by every individual and it should not be misconstrued as a negative trait. Some of the techniques to overcome struggles are as under:

Negative Circumstances Converted into Positivity

If one thinks that life is only a bed of roses, then he or she is surely living in a fool's paradise. To know any great personality in totality, it is essential to read his or her biography to realise the adversities of his life. The story about one's power of endurance is mostly unknown to the world. Remember, hard work means loneliness but it is this to which success is connected. Everybody has to fight his own battle, be it big or small. The larger point is that adverse circumstances lead you towards a positive path, willing you to find the way. It gives an opportunity to resurrect your own life trampled by rigors of troubled times. A successful man is created by encountering failures; so don't get bogged down by failures because success will come knocking on your door, someday or the other.

Auto Suggestion

It is one of the scientifically proven techniques known as the 'placebo effect'. Indulge in self-talk and when feeling low, steer the mind away by saying, 'I have to face it and I will come out of it successfully.' This will help in increasing the willpower when the world seems to be a wretched place to live in.

Whenever negative feelings engulf you and you find life disheartening, imagine yourself as a boxer, while recounting a slogan by James Corbet:

Fight one more round when your feet are so tired that you have to shuffle back to the center of the ring.

Fight one more round, when your arms are so tired that you can hardly lift your hand to come on the ground.

Fight one more round, when your nose is bleeding and your eyes are black, and you are so tired that you wish your opponent would crack you on the jaw and put you to sleep.

Fight one more round, remembering that the man who always fights one more round is never whipped.

Move Past Your Past

No success is final and no failure is fatal. It is an ongoing process. Never lose heart because of the past let-downs and at the same time never become complacent at your triumphs. However, it is always good to derive confidence in your earlier achievements when feeling low. Always keep faith in your fighting abilities and improvise your strategies as per the demands of the situation. Derive inspiration from your own handling of a past critical situation. In short, get rid of your mental blocks and take cues from your intuitive abilities to deal with a problematic issue.

Take the Job Head on

As is often said, Attack is the best form of defense. Taking it further, fire in your belly is the ammunition needed to fight the negative state of affairs and aggression acquires a positive connotation. The desire to face the job head-on must be incited as a behavioral trait. The attitude of embarking upon an action-oriented approach to achieve success must become an intrinsic part of your character.

If there are no hurdles or obstacles, it means either life is very dull or life is devoid of color. Don't shy away from adverse circumstances; face them to emerge stronger than before. Be inspired and try to be an inspiration as well. A man is as good as dead without a struggle.

'Aggression and struggle within self are necessary ingredients for success.'

Be Optimistic

"Life is not a 'tiny candle'; it is a splendid torch that should burn as brightly as possible before being handed over to the next generation."

—Bernard Shaw

Our life is a struggle and full of strife. Every day, there is a new challenge to encounter. When one problem is over, another one knocks at the door and the struggle seems everlasting. But then, no problem is perpetual and all of them have some solution or other. Man is the nerve center of all actions, depending on how he behaves under adverse circumstances and deals with each situation. It is analogous to the situation faced by Abhimanyu in the *Mahabharata*. When he got caught in the maze, he was put to many tests, but yet emerged unscathed. He never lost heart. The moral of the story always is – be *optimistic* till the very end.

To understand optimism better, let's learn about a real example of how it can help in solving a problem.

A person known to me got a heart attack and got himself admitted to the hospital. After some time, his systems slowed down and finally the doctors declared him dead. He was covered with a white sheet, while a colleague of ours stood beside the body, wondering how such an untimely death came about. Suddenly he felt as if there was a vibration inside the white cover and faint ray of hope emerged. He summoned the doctors to check and to our surprise, my friend was indeed alive and continues to live to this day. So keep up your hope, your optimism as it can help to the extent of a dead person coming back to life.

Are you optimist by nature? Here is a simple way to gauge your level of optimism: How do you see half a glass of water? As half full or half empty?

- How do you see the half-moon? Does it seem to be a waxing moon or a waning one?
- How do you pass your night? As the time to sleep and relax or as the eve of the coming morning?
- How you treat a problem? Do you see a solution ahead or as a problem that keeps on troubling you? An optimist finds a solution to every problem.

Mahatma Gandhi said, 'Man often becomes what he believes himself to be.' If I keep on saying that I cannot do a certain thing, it is possible that I may end up becoming incapable of doing it. On the contrary, if I have the belief that I can do it, I shall surely acquire the capacity to do it even if I may not have done it in the beginning.

Why should you be an optimist?

A person is likely to adopt a concept or an idea only when it appears advantageous to him. Keeping this concept as a backdrop, let's see the advantages of being an optimist.

- Better health and happiness
- Ease in working and achieving success
- Better acceptability in society
- Desire to live

(1) Better health: As one traverses through adulthood and advances in age, he starts worrying about his health. This is because, by this time, he would have reached a sound financial position, ensured good schooling for children, acquired a comfortable home, but his health starts deteriorating due to aging. If he has an optimistic outlook, the latter's effect on his health increases. Optimism takes the person on a positive orientation towards the future, which in turn affect his beliefs and behavior.

Happiness is the most intrinsic aspect of human nature and hope is the primary condition that leads to happiness. Optimism is a fundamental cognitive condition that spawns hope, and in turn, reinforces confidence, leading to a pleasant, happy and optimistic life. Hence, it is essential to have more faith while aging.

Dr. Benard Lown, M.D., a Nobel Prize winner for his book, *The Lost Art of Healing*, mentions, *'Faith and optimism have life-giving qualities.'*

Hippocrates, the Father of Medicine, said:*'Some patients, though aware that their position is perilous, recover their health simply through their contentment with the physicians.'*That comes from trust, which a doctor promotes by conveying optimism.

A new study conducted by researchers at the Psychiatric Centre, GGZ Delfland, Delft, The Netherlands, suggests that highly optimistic people have a lower risk of all-cause death and cardiovascular death than those with high levels of pessimism.

The team led by Erik J. Giltay and colleagues analysed the data from the Arnhem Elderly Study to test whether participants who are optimistic live longer than those who are pessimistic.

From the above, it was scientifically proved that optimism reduces all types of health hazards and improves health. So why not build up optimism if not endowed with it?

(2) Ease in work and more success: It a known fact that a man with optimism has a less personal ego and finds himself better placed than others. He receives cooperation from seniors and subordinates in getting a job done, overcoming impediments and resistance. This leads to greater success. An optimistic person can always get help more easily from others than a pessimist can. A pessimist often leaves a job undone, as soon as some hurdle crops up, under the excuse that why he should trouble himself with the problem when he can just avoid facing it. On the other hand, an optimistic person would try to tackle that hurdle with the thought, 'Let me attempt once more'. This 'once more' syndrome is the key to success.

(3) Better acceptability in society: As per Maslow's theory of needs, social recognition is one of the premier needs of mankind. An optimistic person often garners more respect in society. People see him in a glowing light; his words are valued by others. People look towards him to solve their problems because an optimistic person always strives to find a solution. People like to talk to such a person as he inspires others. They tend to get energised on talking to him.

(4) The desire to live: As mentioned earlier, our life is full of struggle. Day in and day out, we have to deal with difficult situations and very often, some of us break down thinking that life is a burden. Under such circumstances, an optimist would never give up; instead, he would treat the situation as a challenge and fight back. An optimist enjoys the life given to him. He not only generates desires within himself but also inspires others to live and enjoy.

There are other numerous advantages of harboring an optimistic attitude. But some may argue that in an environment of challenges, frustrations, and struggles, how can one remain hopeful?

How to Develop Optimism

- **'The future belongs to those who believe in the beauty of their dreams.'**
- **'Optimism is the faith that leads to achievement. Nothing can be done without hope or confidence.'**
- **'You see things and ask, 'why?' but I dream of things and ask, 'why not'?'**
- **'When one door of happiness closes, another opens.'**
- ***'The harder you fall, the higher you bounce.'***

Caution: Optimistic persons need to be warned about becoming overconfident and complacent:

'Keep your eyes on the stars and your feet on the ground.'

Optimism means expecting the best, but confidence means knowing how to handle the worst. Never make a move without weighing the pros and cons just because you happen to be an optimist.

—The Zurich Axioms

After knowing the advantages and precautions, it is essential to know the different techniques for practicing optimism. Some of them are as under:

Learn from yesterday, live for today, hope for tomorrow: Every day is a new day and the previous day becomes the past, while the coming day becomes the future. Every day is a new day for us, requiring to be handled with optimism. It should not bear the shadow of yesterday. Generally, our yesterdays or months and years overcast the present, consequently disturbing our life. It is better to learn from yesterday, our past and live for today, hoping for tomorrow.

Living in Present: Consider every moment as the new moment that requires to be lived accordingly. The present is the moment which needs to be lived before it becomes past.

Dawn follows Dusk: Life does not always follow the same pattern and ups and downs are bound to come. Optimistic persons see the light after every darkness and wait for it with the hope that they will travel on the journey of life and ultimately with hope and optimism, achieve the required result. Believe firmly in the fact that dawn follows dusk; some nights are longer than others, but dawn will always arrive. The need is to observe patience.

It is not the end of life: End of life happens only once, which is, of course, not in our hands. But before that, generally after meeting failure, we tend to feel that it is the end of life and that we shall not ever gain anything in life or that despite all my labor, nothing will be the end result. Such pessimistic thoughts shall not in any way retrieve the situation; they can only aggravate the problems in future. It is not the end of the world or life. Total future may lie in front of you but failures are not permanent; tomorrow you may succeed.

Take inspiration from the following quote:

"I've missed more than 9,000 shots in my career. I've lost almost 300 games 26 times, I've been trusted to take the game's winning shot, but missed. I've failed over and over and over again in my life and that is why I succeed."

—Michael Jordan

Future is bright: Last but not the least, the past may have been a bitter experience, the present is today and tomorrow is unknown to us. Be more hopeful than earlier. Why not think about the brighter side of the situation? With the hope that the future will be brighter, take life in your stride, being optimistic.

So the decision is yours – be optimistic, be happy.

Positive affirmations: We are an embodiment of Energy. The words we speak emanate as vibrations and energy. Positive Energy has a lot to do with the positive, affirmative usage of words. Instead of saying "I don't want to fail", one can say "I want to succeed". Instead of "I don't want to fall sick", it can be "I want to be healthy or I m healthy".

"Yes, I Can and Yes I will" – which is the strongest and most affirmative of all statements. Speaking to your inner mind and often telling it, the right and affirmative words, phrased in the Positive, Present, and Personal tense.

Let us make these positive affirmations as our integral part:

- **I am Happy**
- **I am healthy**
- **I am wealthy**
- **I am worthy**
- **I am hopeful**
- **I am helpful**
- **I am humble**
- **I am blessed**
- **I am thankful**
- **I am grateful**
- **I am unique**
- **I am intelligent**
- **I am kind**
- **I am courteous**
- **I am confident**
- **I am courageous**
- **I am loving**

- **I am caring**
- **I am honest**
- **I am hard working**
- **I am valuable**

On a fertile land, plants have to be sown and nurtured whereas weeds grow by themselves without nurturing. Your mind is like a garden. If you do not deliberately plant flowers in the form of positive and cultivate carefully, weeds in the form of negative thoughts will grow without any encouragement at all. **So positive affirmations and internally speaking to self in a positive manner are necessary to nurture a positive mind.**

Nuggets

- Develop traits leading to a winnable positive personality
- Talent alone is a waste without desire to achieve / succeed
- Imbibe positive desire from early life
- Be Aggressive to take on life's struggles.
- Optimism leads to hope, energy, liveliness, and success, which in turn, lead to happiness.
- Mantra of an Optismist to success– Think Positive, Think Possible, Think Options, Think Solutions
- Failures lead the road to success
- Speak to self in a positive manner to nurture a positive mind

"The greatest discovery of my generation is that human beings can alter their lives by altering their attitudes of mind."

—William James

Notes

(I am being Positive)

Pen down your thoughts/experiences –

Takeaway –

Power of Magnetic Positive Words

1. When someone ask you to do some works what comes to your mind?
2. How many times do you use 'no'?
3. Do you remember three events of the last six months that went off well?

Communication is like two-way traffic – on one side the speaker takes out the word from his/her mouth and on the other side, it is received by the listener. There is a chemical reaction in both the minds and this can be seen through medical experimentation. So it is necessary to speak with caution and whenever required, it is better to utter words from the 'positive'-word inventory that is stored in the mind.

Opposites live together like

1. Day-Night
2. Positive-Negative
3. Yin-Yang
4. Sweet-Sour
5. Long-Short
6. Love-Hate
7. Hot-Cold

From the above, it is seen that the second word is opposite of the first one. The impact of the first word is positive, whereas that of the second is negative. The idea is to enhance the area of influence of the first word which negates the second one.

It is also a matter of research if one of the words could remain without the other. Perhaps it would cause an imbalance in Nature, but the issue is to enhance the area of positive words in life and reduce the use of negative words.

Yin-Yang Aspect of Thinking

1. It is necessary to see the sunny side of life so as to define the influences of the negative yin energy and positive yang energy.
2. Negative yin energy and positive yang energy are connected closely with our emotions and our fortune.
3. Sunny side of life is connected to positive yang energy. Positive energy can be accumulated and transformed from negative energy.
4. To solve problems, to realise dreams, it is necessary to move purposefully towards the sunny side of life. One finds the guarantee that everything that one desires will come true, giving all the pleasures of life.
5. Every second turns into a year and if the person expects happiness, he should move towards the sunny side of life, else his chances of finding that world which he wants are lost forever.

Positive Transformation

1. All people get the opportunity to transform their life into happiness and gain all the treasures they desire.
2. Every person gets some sort of an opportunity to do better in life, but only a few take advantage of it.

3. Being happy is the right of every person and happiness can be derived through positivism.
4. It is the right of every person to be positive and happy.
5. The magic of positive psychology guarantees your transformation into a happy, cheerful and successful person.

Impact of Positive Words

1. Positive words and thoughts propel the motivational center in the brain into action.
2. They help in building resilience when faced with life's problems.
3. According to Sonja Lyubomirsky, one of the world's leading researchers on happiness, in order to maintain lifelong satisfaction, you should regularly engage in *positive thinking about yourself,* share your happiest events with others and savor every positive experience in your life.
4. Research has shown that mere repetition of positive words like love, peace, and compassion can turn on those genes that lessen your physical and emotional stress.
5. You feel better, live longer and build deeper and more trusting relationships with others, both at home and at the workplace.
6. As Fredrickson and Losada point out, when you generate a minimum of five positive thoughts to each negative one, you'll experience 'an optimal range of human functioning'.

   The most powerful word is 'yes'.

New Days of the Week

Let us think differently, instead of following the beaten track.

Let us rename the days of the week and whenever somebody asks for the day, we should inform them of the renamed form. Notice the changes in your personality, thinking, and your health.

Conventional Day	New Positive Day	Action to be Taken
Monday	Motivational Day	Be Motivated.
Tuesday	Tolerance Day	Maintain Tolerance.
Wednesday	Winning Day	Try to conclude things in your favor.
Thursday	Thinking Day	Give proper time to thinking.
Friday	Focus Day	Develop a focused approach to work.
Saturday	Satisfaction Day	Derive satisfaction from tasks fulfilled during the week.
Sunday	Summary Day	Being holiday, dedicate the day to summarise different activities undertaken. Complete the incomplete tasks and find satisfaction in the lessons learned during the week. In case of any shortcoming, corrective action can be taken in the following week.

Positivity since Childhood

'Man should not be differentiated by caste, creed or color, rather on the basis of how he thinks – positive or negative.'

When one takes birth, he is unaware of his caste, creed, color, nation, etc. The society makes him realise all these aspects as he grows older. Gradually he learns to *differentiate*. He also starts learning to say 'no', as the parent always tells him not to do one thing or the other. He hears most of the time in the conversation with him or with others that *something or the other should not be done.* It is sufficient to program the subconscious mental software, which controls the conscious mind and by the time one attains adulthood, one gains sufficient capability to convert a *'yes'* into a *'no'*.

Sometimes I feel, had the word 'no' not been invented, the mental disposition of every person would have been in the *affirmative mode*. How many times have we asked our children on the help extended by them to someone else? How many times do parents ask their children to *try and try again,* instead of scolding them on scoring low marks in their examinations?

So the issue is our training and coaching of our children and *developing an eco-system* at home as well as at school and in society so that the children receive affirmative signals always.

In order to build positivity, we need to unlearn and relearn alphabets learned during childhood. New alphabets are introduced as under:

Sl. No	English Alphabets	Positive Words in English
1	A	Attitude, Assertiveness, Aspirations, Achiever
2	B	Belief, Brand, Boundary Management
3	C	Courage, Concentration, Character
4	D	Desire, Determination, Dream, Devotion
5	E	Effort, Extra Mile, Encouragement
6	F	Focus, Fire in the Belly, Freedom from Fear, Forgive
7	G	Goal, Great, Genuine

Sl. No	English Alphabets	Positive Words in English
8	H	Hope, Happy, Harmony
9	I	Inner Strength, Inspiring
10	J	Justice, Joy, Jubilant
11	K	Keenness, Knack, Knowledge
12	L	Listening, Leadership, Love
13	M	Manage, Motivation, Marvelous
14	N	Noble, Network,Nurture
15	O	Optimism, Outperform, Opportunity
16	P	Positive, Passionate, Perseverance, Purpose, Plus Approach ,Progress
17	Q	Quality, Qualified, Quest
18	R	Role, Responsibility, Relax
19	S	Success, Strength ,Smile, Solution
20	T	Thinking, Tolerance, Team, Transformation, Truth
21	U	Unbiased, Utilisation, Understanding
22	V	Value, Victory, Valiant
23	W	Win, Will Power, Wonderful
24	X	X-cellence, X-factor
25	Y	Yes, Yield, Yearn
26	Z	Zeal, Zest, Zing

If we speak such words in our day-to-day conversations, like instead of saying T for tomato, we say T for tolerance, such words internally affect the subconscious mind of the individual, changing the thought process. Suppose the letter 'Z' is used to say 'zeal', whenever you speak this word, you will be filled with zeal within.

Thus, begin using these new weekdays and new meanings of alphabets.

Use of positive words throughout the day can also be taken as therapy for building a positive mind. Some of the words, which can be used are as under:

Positive Magical Words (21-Day Therapy)

Day 1	Day 2	Day 3	Day 4	Day 5	Day 6	Day 7
Action Achieve-ment Aspira-tion Assertive Appreci-ate	Belief Better	Convic-tion Com-passion Cheerful	Deter-mina-tion Devo-tion Dedica-tion Disci-pline	Extra Mile Efficien-cy Excel-lence Empa-thy	Focus Forgive	Good Goal Great

Day 8	Day 9	Day 10	Day 11	Day 12	Day 13	Day 14
Hope Happi-ness Help	Indomi-table Invinci-ble Inspir-ing	Justice Jubilant Joy	Kind Leader-ship Love	Magnifi-cent Marvel-ous	Noble Never Say No Opti-mism Oppor-tunity Option	Positive Passion-ate Prog-ress

Day 15	Day 16	Day 17	Day 18	Day 19	Day 20	Day 21
Perse-verance Pa-tience Prepa-ration Quest	Righ-teous-ness Relax	Smile Success Strength Solution	Team Truth Toler-ance Trans-forma-tion	Unbi-ased Value Victory Valiant	Win Will-power	Excel-lent Yes Zeal

Note : There may be other positive words, which could be repeated. Readers may write the same.

Repeat these words as much as you can and after some time you will find:

1. These words haunt your mind, i.e. they enter the subconscious mind to replace the negative words.
2. Whenever someone comes to you, you begin to look for reasons to help him.
3. An easy solution to problems.
4. Enhancement of the area of forgiveness.
5. Enhancement of happiness index.
6. Improvement in general health.
7. Development of an affirmative mindset.

So why not to be positive and more positive?

Nuggets

- Share and spread happiness through positive words
- Inculcate positive habits in children at early stage – Start with Positive words
- Start 21 days transformation positive change therapy

"Happiness is not a station you arrive at, but a manner of traveling."

—Margaret Lee Rubeck

Notes

(I am being Positive)

Pen down your thoughts/experiences –

Takeaway –

"The man who removes a mountain begins
by carrying away small stones."

—Chinese proverb

Delta Transformation

(Soch Badlo, Aadat Badlo, Apne Aapko Badlo)

Abraham Lincoln once said, '*Most folks are about as happy as they want to be.*' Was he implying that when it comes to our happiness, we actually do have a choice? Apparently, yes. Research abounds on the impact of positive and negative thinking on ourselves and others and the potential to transform ourselves by changing our habits and mind.

Most often than not, we hear people say:

- **Our culture is bad.**
- **We need to change our mindset.**
- **How to change others.**
- **It's very difficult to handle people.**
- **We will take years to be like developed countries.**
- **Government is not doing anything.**

And this cycle goes on for years. Pursuing the theory of positivity, I decided to find a solution and the only solution was to '*transform oneself*' because you cannot control yourself, even if you want to do so. It is worth mentioning here that the mind controls our actions and needs to be trained as per the requirements. That is why gurus teach us meditation to train our mind as well to exercise control over the same.

It is also worth mentioning here that it takes years to change the culture of a society or a country. Therefore it is prudent to take 'delta steps' towards the transformation. It is told that to win a big run, one needs to take the first step. It is seen that transformation is a slow process, but delta steps when taken by all, lead to a significant change.

It is a challenge to transform an adult; so it is better to start with children when they are in Class 3-8. I still remember the person who came to our school when I was in Class 8th (1972) and advised us to take tea of *tulsi* leaves and bread made out of the wheat husk. I started the same at that time and still follow to this day.

Keeping the above into consideration, adopt the concept of ***'Soch Badlo, Adat Badlo, Apne Aap Ko Badlo'*** (change thinking, change the habit, change self) because the thinking mind develops a habit and making a habit a routine leads to change in oneself.

Thinking is an important aspect of human behavior. The way we *think reflects our behavior and in turn, reflects in our actions,*thus having a direct impact on the culture and society we live in. This article promotes transformational thinking, which lays emphasis on the need and importance of changing the traditional/conventional way of thinking about certain elements. This, in turn, will go a long way in constituting an evolved, progressive, harmonious and sustainable society for our coming generations. This way we help in the development of community/society/country along with respect for individuals, concern for Mother Nature and careful use of natural resources we are blessed with. Human beings and their style of living are constantly evolving, so it is all the more imperative to adapt and embrace the change so as to exercise a positive impact on the society by building an inclusive environment for all.

It is a transformational concept on the way we think. Our thinking becomes habit and habit becomes our personality. So, the way we think has an impact on our nature and behavior and society at large.

Use of Terms

1. ***Transform Thinking*:** All our actions begin at the mental level. The signals for operating start from the spiritual sphere. Thinking is the function of mental faculties. We need to send a message to our mind for any change that we desire. The steps include acceptance, acknowledgment, and action. Transformation is different to change. Change is the outcome of transformation. Transformation needs practice and perseverance, which is being explained later.

   So, we need to accept and acknowledge our conventional thinking pattern and taking action for transforming the thinking profile.
2. ***Change Habit:*** We are slaves of our habits, which are also a function of our mental orientation. Habits are formed by routine and reward.

Chunking – The Root Cause of Habits

The process in which the brain converts a sequence of actions into an automatic routine is known as 'chunking' and it is at the root of how habits form.

Habits, scientists say, form because the brain is continually looking for ways to save effort. Left to its own devices, the brain would try to make almost any routine into a habit, because habits allow our minds to avoid exertion. *This effort-saving instinct is an advantage.* An efficient brain requires less room, which makes for a smaller head, easier childbirth, and low mortality rate. An active mind allows us to stop thinking about the basic modes of behavior.

Step Loop in Habit Formation

The processing of the mind is a three-step loop.

1. There is a *cue, a trigger* that guides our mind to go into automatic mode and choose the habit to use.
2. Then there is *the routine,* which can be physical or mental or emotional.
3. Finally, there is *a reward,* which helps our brain figure out if this particular loop is worth remembering in the future. Over time, this loop – cue, routine, reward – becomes automatic.
4. Ultimately, a habit is formed.

Does Brain Stop Work?

When a habit emerges, the brain stops to participate fully in decision making. It stops working hard or diverts its focus to other tasks. So unless you *deliberately fight a habit,* unless you find new routines, the pattern will unfold automatically. *This deliberate effort is required for the development of the practice and in helping to control yourself.*

How to Change a Habit?

The loop of 'cue, routine and reward' is helpful in developing a habit and when the routine or reward starts diminishing, the habit will disappear if not well ingrained in the mind.

So if we need to change or transform the self, the requirement is for changing our thinking and habits. *But, why you?*

The issue is simple. Most of the times we blame others or try to sermonise others to change themselves in day-to-day life or blame our circumstances or destiny. In fact, for all our actions, we alone are responsible. So the need is to change ourselves.

Now the total population of the country is a summation of the individual. If about 10 % of the people go for a delta (small) change every year, one can visualise the transformation that would occur in the country and the world at large.

The requirement is to think differently, which will lead to transformation.

Nuggets

- A small change can do wonders in life
- Thinking leads to habit. A habit, if followed regularly, leads to behavior and cumulative behavior becomes a culture.

Notes

(I am being Positive)

Pen down your thoughts/experiences –

Takeaway –

Thinking Patterns

Thinking on any subject is the key to many issues as we live in an environment of uncertainties and turbulence. Thinking pattern solely depends upon two aspects:

- **Perception of the subject**
- **Our thinking pattern**

It all depends upon the individual. R. Gopalakrishnan, Chairman, Tata Sons writes, '*We have known that future will be different from the past. Every science fiction writer, from Jules Verne to William Gibson, has reminded us of that. Our erroneous attitude towards the future is rooted in our culturally ingrained notions of predictability and control, a world in which change appears to be linear, continuous and to some extent, predictable. Linearity is the artificial way of viewing the world because linearity concerns efficiency, not necessary effectiveness.*'

We generally think aerially and not in a zigzag manner and accordingly, we arm ourselves with all the tools to face the issue. But in real life, it does not happen so and one has to be happy with marginal success or failure.

One can take corollary from different patterns in the world. Other than drawing a line on paper, nothing seems to be linear. Many times results are same as thought by us. Whenever results are in favor, analyse your plan, strategy, *thinking pattern*. This world is like a game of chess, wherein moves are always planned in advance and many alternates are required to commensurate with the move of the opponents. Thus, instead of straight thinking, it requires to be changed to a spiral one. Spiral has more momentum than a straight one as due to the spiral pattern, speed gets charged more frequently, thus giving rise to a higher speed. Mostly it is based on experience, reaction of opponents, linked activities, etc.

Generally, the thinking process is driven by mental conditioning contributed by love, fear, and other conditioning elements. Whenever any thought process starts, it revolves around the same mental premise and the outcome is of the same pattern as was thought earlier. Have you thought that you can also think differently?

Write down the decision you have taken during the last month/week and study its pattern to find if it indicates the same pattern or a different one.

Visualise the reaction inside you and in your mind. Some of the methodologies attributing to change in the thinking process are as under:

1. Clarity in Thoughts: Thought is pure energy. The energy of thought never dies. Positive *mental* attitude is a mental state of an individual, which is reflected in day to day activities. It makes one decide on *the objective, plan the strategy and achieve the goal.* It gives rise to the clarity of mind.

All the cobwebs of doubt and disbelief must be removed to achieve transparency of thoughts. All that you want to achieve should be crystal clear in your mind and without any confusion, as clarity of thoughts and objectives are essential for reaching the goal.

2. Develop Intuitive Capability: Intuitive capabilities help in developing a proper thinking pattern. Intuition is soul guidance, appearing naturally in man during those moments when his mind is calm. The cosmos is full of thoughts of every kind and the need is to adopt it and accordingly understand the pattern of the subject. The mind needs to be tuned automatically as per the requirements of the subject. At this point, it is essential to know oneself and thinking patterns.

- ***Think Differently***: One may argue that what is the need for thinking in a different way? But in this life of uncertainty, one needs to think of all the pros and cons before reaching any decision. Sometimes such thinking yields better results. Take the case of negotiation with the opposite party which thinks differently from you. Try to visualise his thinking pattern and place yourself in the same situation before opening a dialogue. Spiral thinking helps to reach the solution, which straight thinking may not help as in spiral thinking, the end is reached immediately after every new step germinates. It helps in developing an open-minded personality.

- ***Accept Turbulences***: One must realise that life is not a straight line, i.e. it has its highs and lows. Despite realising the turbulences, one always finds oneself in the doldrums. Turbulences are bound to occur. One day, when I was hospitalised on account of an ailment, I called my friend to discuss my problem. Instead of asking about my welfare, he replied that it was good for me. I queried him about his reply and he said that such turbulences occur in life and since I had borne it bravely, it wouldn't be repeated shortly. So one should try to recuperate as fast as possible. So, what matters is how you think.

- ***Think of the Planet and Others rather than of Self*:** The planet Earth comprises air, water, trees, and atmosphere. Destruction of the environment and imbalance of Nature is posing a serious threat to the world. This aspect has become important today when global warming is threatening us as the temperature of the Earth is projected to rise by 2 degrees.

Water scarcity is also being projected as a threat. Air pollution in most cities is raising alarm signals. So it has become pertinent now to think about our planet and people apart from oneself. This can happen only when we change our thinking pattern.

- ***Shun Traditional Thinking Pattern*:** Most of the time our thinking pattern on a similar situation happens to be the same. What hampers us to think differently? If we think of sickness or disease, our body will translate these thoughts into physical forms. It is because the inner process of translation of thought is linear, just as we think, we tend to behave accordingly. Is it possible to reverse this linearity and think differently? To be clearer in a situation of ill health.

Transformational Thoughts

***Conventional Thinking*:** It is a pattern of thinking which most people possess.

***Transformed Thinking*:** It's a pattern or process of thinking which converts conventional thinking into an ideology that is more inclusive than self.

Some areas where we need to think differently from conventional thinking/traditional thinking call for transformational thinking.

Self

1. ***Conventional Thinking*****:** It's my time and we believe that we have enough time to do things /activities as per our own will and wish.

Transformed Thinking**:** *Time is precious* and more costly than even money. Try to utilise every moment of your time by its efficient utilisation.

Impact: This way you would be more efficient and have more time to devote to family and others.

Society/Planet

2. ***Conventional Thinking*****:** Water is available in abundance for use and will never get exhausted; hence use water as much as you want.

Transformed Thinking**:** Water is a limited natural resource, especially drinking water. Many villages are deprived of drinking water. It is becoming one of the major issues for future generations; hence the habit of frugal use of water needs to be developed.

Impact**:** Water loss would slow down and will be available for generations to come.

3. ***Conventional Thinking*****:** It is the duty of the Army to protect the borders of the country and the invasion of the State.

Transformed Thinking**:** We must respect the Army. It is because of the Army that we sleep in peace.

Impact**:** It is the way to show respect to the Army.

4. ***Conventional Thinking*****:** There are many problems and difficulties in life, which prevent us from doing things.

Transformed Thinking**:** There are challenges before us and we have to find out ways to overcome them.

***Impact*:** Transforms a person, making him or her a problem-solver. The success rate would get enhanced.

5. *Conventional Thinking*: The government must work towards the welfare of the citizens of the nation.

***Transformed Thinking*:** As citizens, it is our responsibility to follow all rules and regulations

***Impact*:** It would develop a sustainable nation, wherein everyone connects, cooperates and collaborates with government initiatives. It would change the perspective of all. It is our nation, which needs to be built by us.

6. *Conventional Thinking*: We mostly react to the situation instead of understanding the cause and effect.

***Transformed Thinking*:** It is advisable to understand the situation prior to acting. Most of the time one needs to preempt the impact of the action. It should become a habit to understand the risks and take precautionary measures. Before taking action, we should be proactive to handle the situation before the case gets out of hand. One of the proactive actions is to exercise regularly, just as all health healers would advise.

***Impact*:** Helps in developing self-efficiency.

7. *Conventional Thinking*: We are responsible for keeping our house clean.

***Transformed Thinking*:** We should develop and practice cleanliness until it becomes a habit. We should not litter the place outside our house because the cleanliness of the surroundings is no less important. Degradable and non-degradable trash should be segregated, including that meant for composting into bio-degradable trash.

***Impact*:** As explained above, a small action needs to be done by society at large as its cumulative effect will help in the transformation of the community and the country. Habit gradually becomes behavior, which, in turn, leads to culture.

8. *Conventional Thinking*: We have the right to use all the natural resources available at our disposal. Oil is one of the resources which has been exploited since time immemorial. The economy of the community and the country depends on oil, both as exporter or importer.

***Transformed Thinking*:** The natural resources are limited and should be conserved for the future generation. Although we can pay, we should be careful about the use of natural resources. It is better to use natural gas in place of LPG for household purposes and also use it as a vehicular fuel. It would not only save the import cost of fuel but also protect the environment.

***Impact*:** Improvement in the economy of the country would be helpful for its development.

9. *Conventional Thinking*: Electricity is in abundance and we have the right to use as much as we want.

***Transformed Thinking*:** Electricity is produced by oil or gas which is a limited and expensive resource. We should use these very judiciously. If we save 1 unit per day, in Indian perspective the saving would amount to Rs 10,000 crores when all the houses do so. It is better to switch over to solar or other renewable energy resources.

***Impact*:** It would help to generate energy for our generation for a longer time.

10. *Conventional Thinking*: Only boys have the first right to education rather than the girl child.

Transformed Thinking: Education is important for the development of self, community, and society. Everyone has an equal right to education. All parents should encourage their child to study and become literate. It would be possible only after we change our thinking.

Impact: It would help in removing gender bias.

11. *Conventional Thinking*: In my country, it is my law, so I can do as I wish.

Transformed Thinking: Follow the law of the land to constitute a civilised society. It is essential for the development of the country for which we should pay the taxes in time, stop when the traffic light is red, avoid using plastic, desist from spoiling the environment.

Impact: It would make life simple without causing any tension on account of law, develop a disciplined society and help in the welfare of the State.

12. *Conventional Thinking*: We should respect our elders. There are certain families which do not follow this conduct.

Transformed Thinking: An elder is an elder, irrespective of class, creed or color. We should appreciate all human beings and support and help them when in need. When you notice an elder crossing the road, help him to do so or if he is carrying luggage, take his load and guide him to his destination.

Impact: It has a direct impact on the culture of the country and imparts pleasure after helping somebody and fosters a feeling of empathy and inner happiness.

13. *Conventional Thinking*: I have more rights as per the constitution (at the expense of duties).

***Transformed Thinking*:** If all the citizens start thinking about their duties and rights, then none can stop the State from progressing and at the micro-level, the village will also develop and be sustainable. Remember that you have duties along with the rights. It has been observed that the priority of developed countries is 'country first, self later'.

***Impact*:** Development of the society or nation will be faster and sustainable when most people start thinking first about the country than themselves.

14. *Conventional Thinking*: Religion is essential and supreme.

***Transformed Thinking*:** All religions are equally important and should be respected. The faith of every person should be accepted and respected.

***Impact*:** It would foster harmony among different religions, reduce hostility and help in the development of the country.

15. *Conventional Thinking*: To think that I am fit and healthy and will visit a doctor when I fall sick.

***Transformed Thinking*:** Go in for regular health checkups because by being healthy, you will be more happy and productive.

***Impact*:** Better health provides more time for self and the family to lead a happy life. The country which has healthy people is bound to succeed in the long run and be more sustainable.

16. *Conventional Thinking*: In most dialogues, we find that the speaker feels he knows better than the other with whom he or she is conversing and fails to accept the viewpoint of others. This may lead to taking the wrong decisions besides causing disharmony among people. This could occur in the family, the school, the organisation and cause ill feelings.

Transformed Thinking: We should not ignore the other person's views during a conversation or a meeting. Respect for the other's views should be developed into a habit right from childhood only. During a discussion with family members, it is advisable to seek others' views before coming to a decision.

Impact: It would lead to a better decision and be inclusive.

17. *Conventional Thinking*: Sympathy is a feeling of compassion or pity for the hardships that another person is undergoing. We are generally sympathetic to others but refuse to help in any way possible.

Transformed Thinking: It is putting yourself in the shoes of another because then only can we understand the plight of the other and be encouraged to take action to help. For example, a poor child may not be able to attend school due to his inability to pay the fees. A sympathetic mind will feel sorry and induce you to help the child financially or in any other possible way.

Impact: Lead to the development of a better society and nation while spreading harmony and happiness.

18. *Conventional Thinking*: A large % of the population lives below the poverty line in India. In other words, 60 % or 763 million people in India were living below the poverty line in 2011.

Generally, most people either don't have sympathy or pity for the poor.

Transformed Thinking: Empowering the poor is the duty of all, particularly the talented poor students so as to enable them to realise their dreams. To do so, one needs to transform one's thinking process.

Impact: It would help the poor to fulfill their dreams and thereby develop a positive eco-system, where everyone will think about the poor and offer help.

19. ***Food for Health***

***Conventional Thinking*:** Food is for eating and I can eat anything as much as I like.

***Transformed Thinking*:** Every food item has a different nutritional value. We should eat healthy food as per the requirements of the body.

***Impact*:** The food we eat has a direct impact on our physical and mental health. We should eat healthy to stay fit, active and alert.

20. ***Don't Waste Food***

***Conventional Thinking*:** Food is in abundance. I can consume or waste it. This is particularly seen in a hotel or at a marriage party, where the guests fill their plates with food but are unable to eat it all. So they leave behind some items which are either wasted or thrown into the garbage.

***Transformed Thinking*:** Information on food scarcity and its impact are given below:

After a tsunami in Japan, one Indian went to dine out with his family in a restaurant. The steward did not accept the payment as he pointed out that the guests had wasted food. When asked why they had wasted food, the guest replied that they were paying for it and it should not matter to him. The steward called the police who told the family that not only would they have made the payment but pay extra for wasting food as they had no right to waste.

So, better change the thinking process and make an effort not to waste food and also prevent others from doing so.

21. ***Dribbling to Deliver***

***Conventional Thinking*:** I will do the work assigned to me, but would ask others to do it for me. If he or she is not able to do it, how am I to be blamed? I cannot control others. This is called a dribbling approach.

Transformed Thinking: I will complete the work in the given time. To me, the goal is clear along with the time. I will complete the work within the prescribed time. I am focused on the goal.

Impact: Sudden enhancement in the efficiency of self, as well as organisation at the macro level, will be seen.

Apart from the above, there may be many other situations which, if transformed, would lead to a better society, country and the world at large, where harmony, happiness, and progress would prevail.

Nuggets

- Shifting in conventional thinking is sufficient for transformed thinking

Notes

(I am being Positive)

Pen down your thoughts/experiences –

Takeaway –

"Perseverance is not a long race;
it is many short races one after another."

—Walter Elliott

Transformation in a 21-Day Therapy

Life is full of excitement, challenges, opportunities, etc. It is up to us to derive as much benefit as possible. In order to lead a successful life, we need to develop ourselves through continuous gap identification and corrective actions, else we will become obsolete. In this competitive age, the fear of becoming obsolescence is always present.

Keeping the above reasons in view, *'transformation through a 21-day therapy' has been developed.* It can be treated as medicine or tablet which is taken once a day at the time of sleeping to produce beneficial results after the fourth day and by the end of 21 days. You will feel like a new person in the world and consider it as the rebirth of your personality.

Ground rules for this therapy are:

- ***Truthfulness***
- ***Seriousness***
- ***Keeping a copy and pen***

Daily sitting down at 10 p.m. and taking a tablet for the next day. Next morning at 10 a.m., planning for action is done accordingly.

Day 1: Time: 10 p.m.

Background: Today is the first day of medication. Sit calmly with a copy and pen. Note down your background.

- Who you are?
- How was your upbringing, etc?
- Which was the happiest moment of life?
- Which was the saddest point of life?
- What irritates you?

Day 2: Morning at 10 a.m.

- Keeping your background in view, think of transformation and begin your day.
- **Night 10 p.m.:**Generally one remains under an illusion, creating a gap in thinking and in reality. Today we need to identify our strengths and weaknesses and *accept the self on the basis of as it is and where it is.* This is the point from where our life shall take a turn towards a better tomorrow. Identification of strengths and weaknesses in a truthful manner is the first prerequisite. Think for a while as to why one should deceive oneself. Don't hide from yourself as it is the point of self-diagnosis of areas where treatment is required. Make a list broadly under the following categories:
    - *Mental*
    - *Physical*
    - *Financial*

It is essential to begin at zero levels first if we want to start any improvement. Accept yourself for what you are, candidly admit the facts. Note all the points in the diary, based on which the action plan will have to be developed.

Day 3: Morning at 10 a.m.

- Identify the base parameters related to the mental, physical and financial position and accept what you are on this day and move ahead. Accept yourself in totality.
- **Night 10 p.m.:** Confidence is the key to one's personality. You might have encountered some persons who reply to the questions confidently without having the proper knowledge. It is due to their self-confidence. Confidence is generally offset by fear. Most fear, however, is rooted in ignorance. The more knowledge or skill you have in any area, the less frightened you would become.

So identify your areas of fear, list them down and on day 4, begin on the remedial measures to be taken.

Day 4: Morning at 10 a.m.

- Think of the remedial measures you would take to overcome your fears. The simple rule for fear is to 'face it' and avoid any situation that aggravates your fears. Try to develop an action plan so that during introspection at night, you emerge out of your fear and get charged with confidence.
- **Night 10 p.m.:** To be precise, such moments are generally less. So it becomes more important to enjoy a stock of achievements/happy moments, which are like vitamins to be taken along with an antibiotic.

1. These moments need to be identified explicitly, for example, when your boss appreciates you.
2. When your first child is born.
3. When you visit a foreign country for the first time.
4. When you achieve a difficult target.
5. When you get recognition from society, friends, etc.

6. A valuable exercise for developing higher levels of self-acceptance involves drawing up an inventory for oneself.

Note down all these points and use them daily as tablets to be swallowed.

Day 5: Morning at 10 a.m.

- Remember the points that were noted down the previous night and revise them. Recall one happy moment experienced in the day and use it throughout the day whenever you face a difficult situation. It is my experience that as soon as you remember such a day, there is a rapid flow of positive hormones inside the body and this counters the negative hormonal flow that occurs on confronting a difficult situation. You can feel this happening and you can come out of all such difficult situations.
- **Night 10 p.m.:** Now comes the day to determine the most important goals and objectives.

It has been seen that most of us do work without giving much attention to the objective in life. It is necessary to understand that a normal person cannot do many jobs throughout his or her life. The one who understands this at the earliest is the one to achieve milestones in life. So sit calmly and ponder on

1. Short-term goals
2. Long-term goals

When deciding, keep in mind your capacity, capability, etc.

Day 6: Morning at 10 a.m.

- Select at least one short-term and one long-term goal before starting to work on the same. Dream of achieving the goals and direct all your actions/energy towards fulfilling them.

- **Night 10 p.m.:** Review the day's progress, realise the steps taken and enjoy the feel of a successful person. Prepare a time-plan because time is the essence of life. A minute lost is irretrievable; thus saving time is an essential prerequisite.

1. Learn the art of effective utilisation of time.
2. Do not procrastinate as it is an infectious disease, which requires an immediate cure.
3. *Apply the 10/90 rule* wherein10 % of the time taken to plan your activities in advance will save you 90 % of the effort involved in achieving your goals later. The very act of thinking and planning your work in advance will dramatically reduce the amount of time taken to complete the task.

Day 7: Morning at 10 a.m.

- Plan your day and jot the points down in a diary. Prioritise the activities as per the day's requirements.
- **Night 10 p.m.:** Most people are seduced by the lure of the comfort zone. They do not like to be disturbed by any unpleasant situation. Thus their actions are limited because of their desire to remain in the comfort zone. It is like feeling cold and remaining indoors instead of going out and enjoying the chill. But in life, such comfortable situations are available to a few only, who also are not completely successful. A successful cricketer comes out of the crease to hit the ball out to the fence. Thus
- Start taking risks.
- Try to go into the area where no one else has gone.

Day 8: Morning at 10 a.m.

- Decide to leave the comfort zone and note down all such occasions in your diary. It needs careful attention.

- **Night 10 p.m.:** Sit in a cool place and analyse your life. You will find that life has been full of emotions like joy, sorrow, love, hate, anxiety, anger, etc., with fear being an important element. These affect your productivity, efficiency, and effectiveness. Some fears that are experienced are as follows:

1. A child fears getting beaten by his or her father.
2. The wife fears her inability to fulfill her husband's needs.
3. Man fears about the future of his children in case of his death.
4. Loss of money also is one of the causes of fear.
5. The fear of losing the game.
6. The fear of not getting promotions.
7. The fear of not having the capability to operate computers.
8. Fear of not knowing English.
9. Fear of speaking in public.

Remember that fear does not help in accelerating the process; rather it has a debilitating effect.

The final step is to identify the fear points inside you. Let all the fears come out. Take time and note down in the diary.

Day 9: Morning at 10 a.m.

- Decide immediately to shun all the fear points. A fear remains within only up to a point. As soon as its severity is outweighed by the courage to face it, the situation returns to normal. Do not escape from the situation; it is better to face it. In the long run, this enhances one's courage.

1. Visualise yourself like a bird flying in the sky without any resistance.
2. Feel free and enjoy long breaths of freedom.

3. Imagine yourself as a new body with a new spirit who has no fear.
4. Feel yourself being full of energy and youth.

- **Night 10 p.m.:** Can you visualise that one can do everything – no, but if you were to tell a person that you cannot do this or that, you would be perceived as a negative person. It is the easiest thing in life to say 'no' because this liberates you from all the liabilities and offers you plenty of freedom.

The need is to weigh the consequences of saying 'yes' or 'no'. Develop the capacity to distinguish between different situations. There is no danger in saying 'no' to a subject which is of no use; else try to find out how it can be done if it is essential. The change in approach from 'no' to 'how it can be done' shall change your life to a considerable extent.

Day 10: Morning at 10 a.m.

- After resolving to develop the approach on how it can be done, engrave this thought in mind and proceed to work. During the course of the day, whenever such a situation arises, think of how it can be done.
- **Night 10 p.m.:** In a day of 24 hours, a normal person works for eight hours out of which it is merely four hours that he devotes to effective work. You can judge for yourself your own case. The remaining four hours are spent either in gossiping, attending to the mobile or telephone, drinking tea, etc. That is why our productivity is less than that of foreigners, who effectively utilise their time, be it in office, home, etc. So the need is not to waste your valuable time on non-essentials. For doing this, identify the non-essential areas in your life, some of which may be:

1. Gossiping.
2. Reading newspapers.
3. Watching television serials or cricket matches.
4. Telephoning, etc.

In other words, it is like management of time by weeding out non-essentials from essentials, which is no doubt, an art.

Day 11: Morning at 10 a.m.

- Resolve to remain vigilant on non-essentials and avoid wasting time on them. Better note down such instances.
- **Night 10 p.m.:** Review the activities of the day and review your actions on non-essentials, how you have acted and the changes, if any, in your personality based on the measures taken the preceding day. If the measures are not taken, the results too would not be up to the mark. Please note that you are medicating yourself on your development. If you leave the measures in between, some defects are liable to remain.

Day 12: Morning at 10 a.m.

- Feel the inner change in your mind, thoughts, and personality. You will begin to feel more confident and be able to face anybody and any situation. With better utilisation of time, you would become more vigilant on non-essentials and not waste time over them. Better note down such instances in your notebook.
- **Night 10 p.m.:** If the systems are well placed, the success of the individual is assured. Ad-hocism needs to be avoided. Whims have no role in life. Thus try to develop systems which bring about discipline in your life. A normal person spends time either at the workplace or at home.

At the workplace, the following actions can be taken:

- Develop the habit to note down the different tasks to be completed.
- Plan the actions to be taken in the day as it will prove very effective. Concentrate on completing the day's work. Keep a diary where you can note down your days' agenda. On reaching your workplace, note down the tasks to be undertaken by you as well by other individuals working with you.
- Evaluate daily in the morning the talks completed the previous day as it ensures completion of work.
- Inform your superiors on completion of the work or any important issue as it is necessary to keep them in the loop.
- A documentation system proves beneficial in life. Develop a filing system and keep all the papers systematically so that the required document can be retrieved easily.
- Adopt any other system that may be required.

The home is one place, which contributes to the development of one's personality as well as thoughts. Thus systems play an important role and some of them can be:

- System for exercise.
- System for studying newspapers, magazines. Before retiring for the night, develop a system of reading motivational books.
- System for documenting, like

1. General papers.
2. Property-related documents.
3. Financial matters, like tax, etc.
4. Separate medical files for self and family members.
5. Daily activities (if you want to record).

Day 13: Morning 10 a..m.

- Keep in mind to be systematic, take necessary actions for completing the tasks pertaining to your workplace and your home. File all relevant documents and discard old/obsolete documents. Resolve to be systematic from today itself and reflect the same in your daily duties.
- **Night 10 p.m.:** Have faith in self as it is the panacea to all diseases. You might have seen that medicines prescribed by the doctor do not act on the body if you do not have faith in them. In the same way, if you have faith in oneself, there can be no reason for not being successful. This has been my experience and believe me, you can achieve anything provided you have faith in yourself.

Generate a feeling of faith within, so that you can fulfill whatever you want to achieve.

Day 14:Morning at 10 a.m.

- With confidence in self, start your day. Imagine a change within you and you would start to feel as if you are a lion. Step out of the house with this attitude.
- **Night 10 p.m.:** Resolve to take the tablet of punctuality, which most of us lack. We reach office late by 15 minutes or attend a meeting 5 minutes behind schedule. We forget the duties assigned to others. We are unable to give feedback. All these points have an adverse impact on one's personality, whereas its presence gives a tremendous boost to the personality. Develop the habit of taking action well in advance. Reach office 10 minutes earlier when a meeting has been fixed and leave your home seven minutes before time. In fact, not much effort is required to develop this habit, but it is simply due to inertia that one becomes lazy.

Day 15:Morning at 10 a.m.

- You would start leaving home earlier than what you did earlier in order to reach on time and start the day with confidence in self. You will be surprised at the change in yourself. You would begin to feel like a lion and step out with this attitude. Gradually, improvements would be seen.
- **Night 10 p.m.:** In this age, when time is costlier than anything, duties have to be discharged in a systematic manner, else at the end of the day, you would find that the day did not produce the desired results. Thus the capacity to make decisions and determine the choice for completing a task is essential. Attend to most important issues first. Most successful persons have the astuteness of organizing the first things first. To start with, classify the work as under:
- Urgent
- Important
- Not important
- General

Day 16: Morning at 10 a.m.

- Acquire the benefit of the tablet 'first thing first' and started utilising it since the morning itself. The mind would begin processing the data on the pending activities and their order. It is better to note the list down in the diary as it acts like the base on which to begin work and based on the same, the progress can be monitored. On reaching the workplace, begin the tasks by following the order listed as 'first thing first' in the diary.
- **Night 10 p.m.:** The dose of the tablet should develop a passion for work within you. Most people have a

tendency to leave the job halfway. Identify such cases if you belong to this category. Passion is like a fire, which should always be lit with the fuel of desire: the desire to do, to succeed, to achieve, to fulfill. Nothing is impossible in this world.

This fire should not be doused at any cost. The fuel for its burning needs to be developed by you through a change of attitude.

Day 17: Morning at 10 a.m.

- Does this develop an inner drive within you? Don't you get the feeling of winning the world? In fact, the feel of win, success, and achievement in itself marks the beginning of change, which would lead to more success.
- **Night 10 p.m.:** Most of us possess a very low tolerance level. We tend to react violently over trivial issues and spoil the situation. Agreed, some situations may induce a reaction within, but the reaction is a stigma to a good personality.

So, in order to deal with such a situation, count your breath till ten or twenty and calm down. After some time, the situation shall normalise and you will be able to handle it. In fact, man is known for his capacity to develop resilience to stress.

Day 18: Morning a.m.

- On getting ready to have breakfast, you may find that you have not reacted rudely on being served a cold breakfast. The reason could be that your children were getting late to school. Practice developing more stress-tolerance and your personality would begin to shine.
- **Night 10 p.m.:** Besides strengthening the inner capacities, the outer fabric too required developing as

this is no less important. Here, the question of personal magnetism comes into the picture. In order to develop such an attribute, the following points may be kept in mind:

- Daily exercise, meditate or do *pranayama* to strengthen the body.
- Proper clothes as per the requirements of the season and occasion.
- Modulation of speech.
- Knowledge of different subjects.
- Speaking only when required.

Day 19:Morning at 10 a.m.

- By now you may have got into the habit of getting up early in the morning to take a morning walk, for which, wear loose clothes while your mind must be trying to recall the day's tasks that need to be implemented.
- **Night 10 p.m.:** Now comes the last day of therapy which calls for an analysis of the actions taken so far on each day.

The time has come for 'detachment from results', which is generally not as easy as it may seem. We, however, need to strive for it. You may have noticed that when you long for something, it goes far away from you.

Day 20:Morning at 10 a.m.

- Positive results would emerge due to the labor you have put in, but the efforts should be detached from the results. Believe it or not, this will give immense satisfaction as well as confidence.
- **Night 10 p.m.:** Observe any mental as well as physical change in yourself and introspect.

Day 21:Morning at 10 a.m.

- You are ready to start your life afresh. Set your Goals to achieve your targets.

You are bound to be successful. Follow this therapy as many times as you want. Share it with your friends.

"It is not enough to take steps which may some day lead to a goal; each step must be itself a goal and a step likewise."

—Goethe

Notes

(I am being Positive)

Pen down your thoughts/experiences –

Takeaway –

"Don't measure yourself by what you've accomplished,
but rather by what you should have accomplished with your abilities."
—John Wooden

Transformation - Negative to Positive Thinking

A 1° Shift in your thinking process is sufficient to transform your life. It requires delibrate and consistent approach.

So, Let us start!

Now is a time to start a journey for transformation to Think Positive.

Daily Thoughts Reconciliation

Capture the thought before it ripples down as you can never know the potential of the thought.

Thoughts are the mirror of a person's mental status. The mind generates thousands of thoughts per second; some ripple down but some emerge from the subconscious mind. It has been seen that thoughts come and go faster.

The thought is the mental process in which beings form psychological associations and models of the world. Thinking is manipulating information, as when we form concepts, engage in problem-solving, reason and make decisions. The act of thinking produces thoughts.

Author and investor Tim Ferris recommends jotting down the thoughts in a log register every morning and emphasise that writing is more important than the final product.

But the issue is how to capture it. At the first level, remember the thought and when you reach home, write down the same or purchase the Phillips hand recorder, which is a useful device. Whenever a thought arises, record the same. Now, you can use a smart phone to record the thoughts as notes. All these thoughts which have been explained above can be a part of your morning walk.

Start writing your own quotes/daily thoughts emerging during the day and observe the impact they make in your daily life.

Sl. no.	Positive Thoughts	Negative Thoughts
Total		

Net Positive Index = Number of Positive Thoughts /Number of Negative Thoughts

Get a log register for the same and log them.

Next level is to calculate the power of thoughts.

Sl. no.	Positive Thoughts	Weightage	Negative Thoughts	Weightage
Total				

Here, the term 'weight' has been inserted. It is the power of thoughts which determine our actions. It is better to give weight to the thought to calculate the net power of thoughts comprising positive and negative ones.

Net Positive Power Index = Power of Positive Thoughts /Power of Negative Thoughts

Transformation from Negative to Positive frame of mind

Lately I have experienced that it is negativity can be transformed into positivity by deliberateness. It is not a theory or art but a science .

In order to establish this fact ,I did experimentation on some of our associates,advised them to note down the thought process and in particular the negative thought and do following action:

1. Observe the thought
2. Pause for a second
3. Reflect the thought from the mental positive fire wall
4. Send transformed positive thought to sub-conscious mind

Guidelines

1. Before start of the transformation exercise – have open mind to change .
2. You need to observe the thought process .
3. You need to give a auto-suggestion to the mind to change the track of negativity to Positivity
4. Log you thoughts on daily basis in a copy or register .
5. Observe the transformation process from negativity to positivity.

For Example :

Sl. No.	Situation	Negative Thought	Auto – Suggestion	Transformed Positive Thought
1	Can not approach	I "Can not Do / Not possible" to this work, as I have no resources	Why I can do ?	Let me try, I can do

Observe your thoughts as above in a span of 7 days and jot down the results.

Day No.	Date	Situation	Negative Thought	Auto – Suggestion	Transformed Positive Thought
1					
2					
3					
4					
5					
6					
7					

Observation :

I have found following changes within me.

1. ....
2. ....
3. ....
4. ....
5. ....
6. ....
7. ....

Let us go back to set of two Questionnaires given earlier

Negative Quotient:

Rate yourself on the following attributes in a scale of 1 to 10:

Sl. No.	Indicators	Rate out of 10
1.	You often use 'cannot do' or 'not possible' or some such words	
2.	You get easily stressed out while encountering problems	
3.	It is easier to control your associates by highlighting their weaknesses	
4.	You feel disappointed when stressed	
5.	You find things difficult to prioritise when they get accumulated	
6.	The first thought that comes to your mind when a severe problem crops up is to find an escape route	
7.	You often feel burdened while serving others	
8.	You are argumentative to the point of considering yourself right while the others are wrong	
9.	You often hesitate in exploring alternate/new solutions for fear of failure	
10.	You get easily tensed over trivial issues	
11.	You find it difficult to appreciate others	
12.	You get impatient if the task is not completed and have the tendency to leave the job unfinished	
13.	You are fearful of taking decisions	
14.	You do not want to take on an unexpected responsibility	
15.	You get disappointed when things don't work according to you	

Calculate your score:

A.	Total marks	150
B.	Your marks (out of 150)	___
C.	Negative Quotient (NQ) (B/A)*100	___

Positivity Quotient:

Rate yourself on the following attributes in a scale of 1 to 10:

Sl. No.	Attribute	Rating Out of 10
1	Are you generally smiling	
2	Do you remain unruffled when problems arise	
3	Do you have a generally helpful attitude	
4	Are you optimistic and always see a silver lining to every cloud	
5	Do you see a half glass filled or half glass empty	
6	Do you look at strengths than weaknesses of associates	
7	Do you generally act without prejudice	
8	Are you fearless	
9	Do you take decisions	
10	Do you generally look for a solution	
11	Do you extend help to others	
12	Are you generally happy	
13	In case of obstacles and challenges, what is the level of your excitement	
14	Do you like challenges	
15	Do you appreciate others for their goodness or good deeds	
16	Do you inspire others	
17	Do you manage your time well	
18	Do you bounce back after any failure	
19	Are you open-minded on controversial issues	
20	Are you open to suggestions for improvement in your work and willing to go an extra mile to handle extra work	
21	Do you handle stress well	

Calculate your score:

A.	Total marks	210
B.	Your marks (out of 210)	___
C.	Positive Quotient (PQ) (B/A)*100	___

Transformation Index

My transformation Index after reading this book is :

Negativity Quotient (NQ)

Before (Page - 40)	After (Page -160)

Positivity Quotient (PQ)

Before (Page - 68)	After (Page - 162)

You will observe that your thinking process is getting transformed from Negative to Positive.

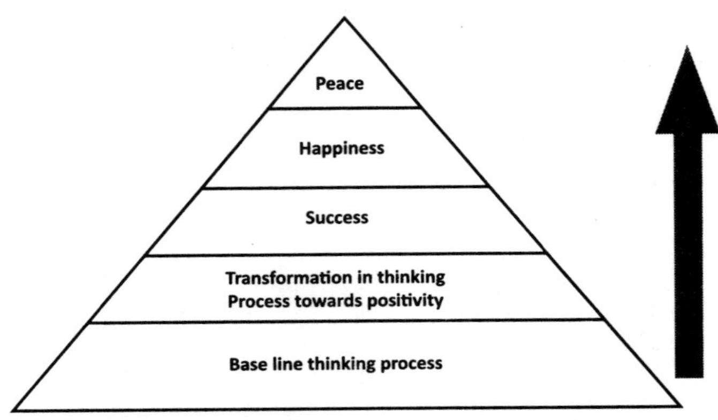

Transformation to positivity leads to Success, Happiness and ultimately to peace.

□

Notes

(I am being Positive)

Pen down your thoughts/experiences –

Takeaway –

5

Real life experiences of Thinking Positive

'I always knew I was going to be rich.
I don't think I ever doubted it for a minute.'
—Warren Buffett, 1930,
American investment entrepreneur

Real life experiences of Thinking Positive

During the course of my life journey, I have come across different people from different backgrounds who have left an indelible impression om me. At the same time, I feel that I have been able to influence some of them with my thoughts.

Here is an excerpt of real-life experiences of some of them:

Harish Bhatt
Founder & CEO, (Community service Group)

*It has been a daily routine to have read the powerful book *"YES YOU CAN"* written by the author. I keep this book close to my heart as it helps me convert my negative thoughts into positive thoughts and always reminds me of positivity in my all day to day actions. I have felt the positive transformation in my life after reading the book *"YES I CAN"*. As a result, now I feel,*

- *I am more focused,*
- *Anger & procrastination have reduced*
- *Patience, health-conscious, discipline has increased,*
- *Proper documentation of important documents i.e. household items has been adopted*

- *Supportive nature has got developed*
- *Target oriented,*
- *Negative communication at home, neighbors, community has reduced.*
- *Now I try to convert negative communication into positive communication & help them also become part of positive communication .*

Whenever I feel demoralised (its human nature), I read this book to change my attitude & approach – this book is one more step for positive life...

After reading the book, I have started doing the following:

1. *Now make list of priorities of a day*
2. *Avoid arguments on small issues clothes, food, etc., seek for peaceful environment*
3. *Started morning & evening walks with the wife. During the walk, discuss about household matters*
4. *Keep proper documentation of electricity, water, telephone bills as well as important numbers of plumber, electrician, carpenter, car mechanic, etc.*
5. *Ignore negative communication at home, neighbors, community and try to convert negative communication into positive communication & help them also become part of positive communication because with negative communication no gain, only increases stress, poor health & poor relations with others i.e. family members, neighbors, colleagues in office.*
6. *Interact with members of society, understand their hobbies, problems, take group decisions for support, developed reading/recreation room, put dustbin for the cleanliness of compound, plantation for greenery,*

Andrea Vattuone
Director (RINA Consultant)

Whenever you start thinking positive you will be able to change your behavior towards other people and yourself. Positivity always comes with kindness. Behaving positively and kindly towards people in most cases provides kindness back and whichever thing seemed not achievable in principle may not be like that anymore.

- *I was waiting for some documents at the counter but was getting frustrated with lack of proper response from my the concerned officer. However, thinking positive and acting kindly enabled me to obtain what I needed.*

Never give up. This is the most important lesson I have learnt, in any situation of your life. This does not mean that you need to achieve ultimately everything at any cost, but that you will have to act at the best of your capabilities and spend your most genuine efforts to reach your goal despite the adversities.

- *I was playing tennis and was at first set point after 2 hours fight with my opponent. I lost the set and had to start all over again, in an inferior position after such tiring efforts.*

That is the moment in which you win or lose the match. Only through positive thinking, I fought with all my will and won.

- *I live in a different country from my native one. This gives me the chance to meet a lot of new people and at the same time, feel incredibly lonely. Positivity is the changing factor allowing me to make friends with people I meet.*

A positive attitude provides me the mental strength to know that whichever will be the challenge I will have to face, I will try my level best to succeed. If I will not succeed, not such a big deal, I will train/study/prepare better and will succeed.

Abhimanyu Singh, co founder of iCONEX

I am Abhimanyu Singh, co founder of iCONEX in India, Bahrain and USA, along with Tech Eight Consultancy in Dubai. iCONEX is growing at a breakneck speed and since its inception in June 2015 with only 3 people on board; has become 52 member team in 52 months. People from different countries and different continents work and iCONEX is looking forward to become first Multi National from India in the field of organised oil and gas corporate events and will be achieving the mark of USD 15 million by the end of next year.

But, the growth of iCONEX was not possible if I didn't have the Positivity ... Positivity which got injected to me through a book "YES! I CAN". It so happened like during new company formation you go through a lot of strain and initial business rinses you off financially and emotionally. But a positive behavior changes everything. I wanted to read something good and on Kindle; I found this book, which had 5 stars, I started reading curiously as generally we don't get to see a 5 star rating for Indian writings. As I went through the pages, It gave me strength to stand for myself in that time of adverse conditions.

Even today as business cycle moves and you feel like giving up to certain situations, I reopen the book. Take any chapter. It takes me out of the situation and changes my approach to challenging situation.

I met Dr. Karnatak almost after a year I had read the book. The moment I can never forget, that I was meeting the person who had changed my approach to all the problems. Not only in present, in future too. This book is now my bible. Answers to all the challenges I face. Always with me. Thank you Dr. Karnatak, you must have changed lives of millions... I am just a drop in the ocean.... Thank you once again.

Ashish Verma

Director (SAP- Consulting services)

As a result of Thinking positive, I have observed following changes in self –

- *Behaviour has turned more receptive and open to people and ideas*
- *Approach has turned to more constructive and problem solver then problem pointer*
- *Delivery index – Bar has been raised from average to above average*

Social life has taken a new turn, most of the negative influence people are either not my contacts or no more in my 'First circle' of social activity. This has led to lesser number of friends. Having said that it has opened a new door to extended social life wherein even a stranger can be turned into a friend. Not a friend of need / for need but a true friend.

Life is very short if you are joyous and very long of you are not.

With happiness in your heart, days fly into weeks, weeks into month and months into years wherein time flies faster than what one can comprehend. Many areas have been impacted i.e overall relationship whether personal or professional, views towards situations, people and instances has been upgraded, a beautiful support system has been involved within myself which I can look upon and consult for any area of my life.

It has made me More than a Super Human- i.e it is Super in itself to be Human.

S. Ravishankar
CEO (Procube Project Consultants LLP)

Transformation comes from within – A personal experience

Transformation is a journey. *I realise that I am still on that journey. There is no finishing line. It is not just change. Everyone changes as one grows old, progresses in her or his career, travels through the family life but that's is not transformation. Then what is transformation to me? It is progression from one level to another level and again to the next level. Personally, I started seeing transformation in myself, when I started defining, rather redefining my life, started taking actions towards my goals without getting influenced by others or going by what others say or following the crowd.*

There are small but significant experiences (significant from my point of view) that started taking place early in my career. These little events started to redefine my approach and ultimately launched me into the journey of transformation.

- *6 years into my career and a couple years after my marriage, I thought I am capable of doing more or I should be doing something more productive than what I was doing as part of my work and decided to do my CFA as an add-on qualification though I had an MBA from a premier institution. My idea was that a deeper understanding of finance will help me later in my career though I was not very sure about the immediate benefit in my current career nor the PSU company in which I was working at that time would give me any special recognition for doing such a course. My wife was very supportive and encouraging and she was quite happy about using my free time to acquire a prestigious qualification. She said to me "If you decide to do something, you will go all out and achieve it, so go ahead". One of my friends said in clear terms to other friends (his intention was to make me hear his words though I was a little away) – "What is the point of adding up a qualification, it does not give any advantage in our company and it is a sheer waste of time". One of my relatives asked me whether the company would give me any increment or promotion,if I complete the course for which my answer was 'No'. Fortunately the deep interest and excitement of doing a good course and completing it, was much stronger than the logically negative comments given by others around me. Yes, I went ahead with the course (that was in 1993 when I was 30) and completed it in little more than the minimum required time period of 3 years – cleared all groups in first attempt. What did I get in my company – no promotion, no increment but ironically I got transferred against my wish from Baroda to Kolkata, a lowly placed regional office in terms of business – alas...my friends were right???. Lets look at what I got out of it – great confidence because I could complete such a difficult course clearing the groups in first attempt; my wife's support and her belief in me; CFA institute started an MBA programme in various cities including Kolkata and I was invited to offer a full programme in marketing as a Visiting Faculty and I was rated as one of the best professors in that year!!!; when I decided to change the job and went for the interview in a new company, the interview board was so impressed with my qualification and my relevant experience that they immediately offered me the job; once I joined the new company in their marketing department to take up responsibility of their upcoming new petrochemcials product, they asked me to review the complete finance and profitability model of their new petrochemicals business because of my background and asked me to present it to the Board of Directors. That presentation made to the Board was a turning point of my career – because all Board members were so impressed with my presentation and extended all support to make the new project a success and I had started the new job putting the best foot forward. My new qualification truly helped me and opened up so many opportunities.*

What was the learning, to name a few?:

- *If you are convinced about doing something useful, trust your instincts and go ahead. Do not get influenced by "What others say". They will logically argue you out of your progressive thinking by talking about the absence of short term benefits,*
- *Any thing you do or any new initiative you take – some may give immediate benefits and some may give long run benefits. More than anything else, studying a good course builds up your knowledge and perspective enormously which cannot be quantified. It helps you at various points in time in your career, which I experienced in my case*
- *It opened up a new opportunity of being a Visiting Faculty, which made you realise the new dimension of your personality and stepped up your confidence in presenting and communication, which is an important skill to acquire as you move forward in your career.*

- *The other experience I would like to talk about is my sudden transfer to Kolkata as mentioned above. It was in 1996, when I was about to complete my CFA and it was indeed a shock to me and my family when I got the transfer order since my plan was to move into finance function from marketing in my current location – Baroda to leverage my newly acquired finance qualification. But the transfer upset my plans and I felt so disappointed. When some friends made fun of the transfer, adding to my misery, I decided that I must meet a GM of my company, who was close to me and who always had been a great well wisher of me. I went and met him. he spoke to me for half an hour, adviced me to cool down, suggested me where I should stay and told me that I will have a great time in Kolkata. That 30 minutes transformed me. Family was again very supportive and we went to Kolkata. The best time of my life was in Kolkata – lot of opportunity to introduce new initiatives since the office itself was a bit laid back, my daughter's early education started in one of the best schools, my visiting faculty stint stared there and an opportunity to handle new areas like product sales and distributor management and creating more efficient systems and processes. When I decided to change my job and applied for GAIL manager position, the Petrochemicals Business Head of GAIL who knew my senior in the company in which I was working in Kolkata, called him and enquired about me and my senior colleague gave an exceptional feedback. My job and career change happened.*

What was the Learning?:

- *You need a right mentor and a mastermind network to guide you whenever you face a challenge. A good immediate family support system is very essential to take you through the challenges.*
- *A mentor and advisor is one who believes in you. Similarly, if you go to someone whom you trust, they*

can be game changers in your life as you have faith in that person.

- *Certain things in life happen which are beyond your control. If you have a positive attitude and move forward, leveraging your strengths, nothing can stop you. In the hindsight, you will realise that what has happened is for your good. You can connect the dots looking backwards and not looking forward. Hindsight almost always defines why something has happened to you in the past. But a positive attitude alone will make you realise the goodness in what has happened in the past.*

- *One final defining experience I would like to share here is the influence of two important ideas that made me take some important successful career moves. During the late 90s, I bought a book by Napoleon Hill titled 'Think and Grow Rich' from a roadside shop in Mumbai. The topics covered in the book added the much vigour and clarity to my action towards attaining my ambitions and goals. The first idea is the Power of Mind. Feeding positive thoughts into your mind can truly energise a person. In short, Success starts from the mind. New ideas start from the mind. What you do those ideas is what determines your success or failure. Adding positive thoughts and imagination to the idea and developing and taking action leads to success. In the process, imagine about success in your mind, add positive affirmations through auto-suggestion and take decisive actions – Success would be on its way. Success is, in short, Idea + Imagination + Action. This core idea of Napoleon Hill had a great impact on me and has over the years become an integral part of my thought process and action. In Hill's words, "Whatever the mind can conceive and believe, it can achieve". Here too, I have lots of little personal experiences to share. But for now, I will leave the readers with the idea described above, to ponder on.*

The second idea which had a great influence on me is what I obtained from webinar on success – 10X thinking. The speaker articulated the idea very well. It is basically thinking big – again it starts with the mind and so it is an extended idea of the Power of Mind. I am still in the process of expanding my thinking and that way, there is no finishing line – lot more to learn here. That's why I call 'Transformation is a journey'. Here two important things required to expand your thinking is : Move away from safety first principle and get out of your comfort zone; The other aspect is to keep the right company who are positive thinkers and achievers – a sort of Mastermind Network.

Dr. Bharat Lohani
Professor & Founder Director
(IIT Kanpur & Geokno India Pvt. Ltd)

Positivity and Negativity are both parts of our life and we keep swinging between these two extremes. The most important transformation comes to one when one becomes conscious of his/ her state of being in any of these two states. Once we realise about our state we also realise that these states are just matter of our thought process and can be altered. A situation can lead one to negativity while the same situation can become impetus to other to seek a positive path. However, this transformation is not a simple process but comes with practice.

I hail from a moderate background where thinking big was a chimera. Maintaining status-quo was important as that would ensure survival. However, seeing a few positive persons around and their deeds provided me the impetus to dare to think bigger and beyond bounds. The belief, that some others could do it by following a positive path, was sure a recipe to keep believing and keep working. The results do happen. I would not rate my achievements very high but I am satisfied that I could make some positive contributions to things around me. I know the journey ahead is full of challenges but I have learnt to tell myself – सब हो जाएगा; हर समस्या का हल है और मेरे आसपास ही है;बस लगे रहो.

Ashish Shukla

(Middle management executive), Marketing, OIL & GAS

"I am a firm believer that positivity is one of the basic prerequisites for living a good and fulfilling life. A person may have all the worldly comforts but still not happy if he is not positive in his thoughts, words, and deeds. Though it's a natural trait for many people who always look at the brighter side of life, many individuals develop it with time from their experiences and see the benefits both physiologically and psychologically. Sooner one gets blessed with the virtue of positive thinking, the better the life becomes for that individual.

Thinking Positive has helped me improve my behavior not only in trying times but also in day-to-day dealings. Thinking Positive has made me a better professional by improving my way of looking at things from a larger perspective. My relationship with co-workers has improved. Also, at the personal front I have improved as a person and try to look out for good qualities rather than finding faults in others.

Life is not understood for what it is but what one wishes it to be. That was my problem. Like many people, I wanted things my way. Though it is true to an extent to wish and try for the things that you feel good about the outcome cannot be guaranteed. I could not accept failure, which is one of the two outcomes for any endeavor, the other one being success. Sometimes even if you miss the shot by a whisker then also you have to accept that you missed the target and move on. There is no point to remorse over the result. What matters more is not that you have lost but what you've learned from the loss and whether the lessons learned are helping you in your next venture. The perspective of looking at failures not as some kind of rejection but as a learning tool helped me tide over the bad phase of life.

The goal setting and goal achievement have improved a lot with positive emotions. The harder the goal is the stronger my resolve becomes to achieve it. I have started setting deadlines for the goals and that has helped in converting my dreams into reality. I have also begun to look at not only what is required to be planned but also if the work is going as per the plans. As they say, I plan out the work and then work out the plan.

It is true that the world measures one's worth by the success one have achieved. In that respect, I find myself having more clarity now on what is required to be a noteworthy individual. Earlier I used to care about goals required for personal gratification and had no discerning eye for the aspirations that are equally important as per societal norms. With this change due to looking at the positive side of personal and societal world and their interplay, I find myself more at ease with pressures of the world and the ways to deal with it more effectively. It is visible what I want to achieve in short-term and where I want myself going in the long run.

A man is a social animal and as much as positivity helped myself deal with my personal self, it has helped me improve my social life in many ways. Earlier I used to be more impulsive and judgmental about other people but now I understand that the social behavior of any person is just the tip of an iceberg and I have no reason to label a person and develop views based on that little visible part of his personality. One thing that has left a lasting imprint on my mind is one teaching of the author that the only way to classify people is whether they are positive thinkers or negative thinkers – that is all that matters. If a person is positive, everything else can fall in place and if the person is negative even the good things will not produce the desired results.

S.K. Sahi
CEO, CSRL

In 1994, on 22nd June, I met a very bad car accident in Patna. That time I was at the peak of my consultancy assignment in Delhi and Mumbai. This accident crushed all my ambitions and hopes. My left Hip and urinary system was badly damaged. I could listen doctors talking that I may not be able to walk on my legs. It took me six months to partly get out of hospital and next 6 months was spent in daily physiotherapy. I was not sure what will I do to earn my bread. But I had read about Stephen Hawking, Lance Armstrong and others. I started thinking what is the use of so much reading if I cannot apply on myself. I decided I will not give up and give life a strong second chance. I was on crutches almost for 3 years but even in that condition I travelled to Cochin and MUMBAI by train to finish some assignments. The management of those companies welcomed me as I was prepared to fight. My offices were closed down since I had no money left after treatment.

Gradually, I gained enough strength to give up one crutch. I built my business gradually. I realised that sympathy from society has very little usefulness. It is the brave, who are appreciated. In next 3 years I rebuilt my office.

Though I still limp and often face troubles but now I have built a great organisation -CSRL and manage Super 30 program at almost 22 locations and help about 800 poor students to get admitted in IIT and NIT etc with a success record of over 87% in last 10 years. Nearly 300 people work with me and have support of major corporates in our mission. When I look back to my dark days of pain and struggle, I feel that only way to rid of bad times is by nurturing a strong hope in mind.

Positivity demands not cursing your misfortune rather taking a determined steps for the future. One can recover 10 year of losses in one year.

Sushil Kumar
(Middle management executive)-
City Gas Distribution Company

My Transformation by Thinking Positive –

Yes, I Can concept gives me a starting point to achieve a target by breaking self-made mental boundaries.

Prayas, Ek Aur Kadam (PEAK): Keep on going Step-by-step towards your goal (Don't stop until achieving your Goal)

For personal growth, I have used these concepts and achieved the desired goals:

Health - The real wealth

During annual health checkup in 2012, it was revealed that my blood sugar level, cholesterol level, and triglyceride levels are high. The doctor suggested controlling these abnormal parameters as these are the early warning of diabetes and cardiovascular disease. Following are the details of critical investigations in pathology reports:-

1. *High blood sugar HbA1c:* **6.9** *mg/dl, normal value is considered below 6.0 mg/dl*
2. *High cholesterol level:* **226.0** *mg/dl, normal value is considered below 200.0 mg/dl*

The consulting doctor advised me to control the sugar and cholesterol level immediately. During discussion, she revealed that diabetes is in fact not a disease but occurs due to sedentary lifestyle. For curing this type -2 diabetes, life-long medication required. Immediately concept of YIC came into my mind. I assured self and doctor that I am ready to embrace modification in my lifestyle. The doctor prescribed the following modification in diet, sleeping schedule, etc:-

Wake-up: at 6:00 am

Tea: Green/ black tea without sugar with two marrie biscuits

Workout: Daily 40 minutes brisk walking in the morning

Breakfast: Oats

At 11:00 am: 11 Almonds

Lunch (1:00-2:00 pm): ¼ plate salad, two chapattis, and seasonal vegetable

At 05:00 pm: One seasonal fruit

7:00- 7:30 pm: one cup of vegetable soup

Dinner (8:30-9:00 pm): ¼ plate salad, two chapattis, dal, and seasonal vegetable

Sleep: go to bed between 10:00-10:30 pm and have a minimum of 7 hours good sleep

I followed the advice strictly and modified my lifestyle accordingly. Started walking without any break. YIC always been a motivating factor to start following daily schedule. Even whenever I happened to be on official trips, I walked on airports, railway stations to complete my daily target. Further to achieve the desired outcome, I used PEAK concept i.e. step by step march towards the desired goal. To achieve the target it took me around 9 months and result in Sept- 13 were following:

1. *High blood sugar HbA1c:* ***5.7*** *mg/dl, normal value is considered below 6.0 mg/dl*
2. *High cholesterol level:* ***200.0*** *mg/dl, normal value is considered below 200.0 mg/dl*

Sports: My Passion

I was transferred to another location in March- 14 where my boss inspired me for long-distance running especially Half Marathons (21 KM). In this case also, I used YIC concept for starting long-distance running and participated in Airtel Delhi half Marathon 2014. I completed the run in 2: 23hrs.

2014- Airtel Delhi half Marathon:

To improve performance in half marathons used PEAK concept and in 2015- Airtel Delhi Half Marathon, it took only 2:06 hrs. to complete the run. Since then I am participating in Half Marathons and maintaining similar timings.

Professional achievements

I was a person of introvert personality with a lot of stage fear. I also had a fear in mind that I cannot write and speak good English as I completed my schooling in Hindi medium. YIC concept inspired me to start writing technical articles/ papers and give presentations in office. Slowly using PEAK as step by step approach, I have written and presented following papers in my organisation level and then national level and finally at international level.

1. *2016- My paper on Measures Taken to Control High Gas Loss (Un-accounted Gas) at Indraprastha Gas Limited (IGL): A case study was adjudged second in the Seminars.*
2. *2016-Calibration & Stamping of Natural Gas Meter: Legal Metrological Requirement*
3. *Dec 2016- March 17: Written a case study on "A step towards energy security: The taste of LNG for Indian consumers through execution of mega pipeline project". A certificate received from S. P. Jain Institute of Management and Research.*
4. *March-17: Presented a case study on Gas Measurement issues in CGD industry in 12th Annual conference on City Gas Distribution in India.*

This was a national level conference in which all the stakeholders related to City Gas Distribution (CGD) business were present including CGD operators, vendors/ suppliers, regulators, etc. The presentation was well appreciated by the CGD fraternity.

Later on, Indian Infrastructure Magazine published Article "Meter Measures: Scope for better metering and billing" based on my presentation.

1. *M/s. India Smart Group Forum (ISGF) invited in India Smart Grid Week 2017 (an international conference) on smart cities to deliver a keynote speech on Smart Utilities-City Gas Distribution on automation perspective.*
2. *Recently, I have presented a paper on 'Strategic Measures Taken to Control LUAG in IGL' in a Global Conference on flow metering at Fluid Control Research Institute (FCRI), Kerala.*

All the above are examples of transformations happened in my life during the last 5 years using YIC and PEAK concepts developed by Dr. Ashutosh Karnatak. I feel my ordinary life is changed into a great one giving me a lot of confidence to achieve my goals whether they may be personal or professional.

P.S. Rathore

Motivational speaker

Frustrated story of a common man -Died or survived ????

It was cloudy that day. The Mausam was amazing. It was drizzling slightly.

A person was sitting in Chauffuer driven black colour Mercedes Benz. The Car was moving from Chandigarh, one of the most beautiful and planned cities in India to Delhi, Capital city on broad and beautiful NH1.

The person sitting behind went in flash back, recalling old days, when he had no money to have two proper meal and often had to sleep without food. He used to wait for his brother to come, so that he can go out as there was just one pair of sleepers.

Suddenly, a smile came upon his face. He was finding pleasure in that pain too.

Today this man was so mesmerising that on his single word, CEO and Chairmen of big Corporates jump into burning coal and walk on fire under his instructions.

His eyes were wet and numb.

Suddenly, his driver Badri's sound broke into his thoughts. Sir, Hum Karnal pahunch Gaye. Haweli aa gaye hain. Kuch kha lete hain.

I suddenly awoke. This was my beautiful past .

Now god has blessed me with famous name P.S. Rathore .Motivational speaker.

I just got out of my past. Came into the present.

Got down from car. Went in haweli. News was going on TV screen. It was India TV. And my firewalk news was coming on TV and my statement was running in news. I saw reactions of people, some were saying - Pagal hai. He is mad.

Others were saying, see how can he enhance confidence of people.

I was silent and calm. Was thanking god irrespective of who said what.

I wasn't influenced by good or bad reviews.

If u have seen worst, small talk does not affect you.

Again I came in my car. I asked Badri to let me drive. Rain was over but it was still cloudy. I opened the car roof top. Was thinking of my journey from Calcutta to Delhi while the music was being played.

This journey was planned by god. I had no money. I was staying with my friends near Radha bazaar.

For food, I used to go to Lalbazaar police station. Pl do not take me wrong. Police station had Mess for their constables. I got acquainted with one of them. With his recommendation, I got a chance to have food there on monthly basis. Food was great something 200 rupees for a month. I still miss the food there.

I met a person there. He asked me what do u do. I said doing icwa and CA. He said what is your future plan.

I said will work here later. He said are u crazy. There is no opportunity in Calcutta.

He advised to go to Delhi.

I asked him but how can I go there. I know no body. He said come to me, I stay in Defence Colony. This is my address.

You must come.

I booked my ticket for Delhi without thinking much, wrote exam and caught train. My friend Bhavesh and Nilesh were scolding me. Pata ni kis pagal ne Kya kah diya and ye ja raha hai. Bhavesh is a silent guy. He thinks about friends and believes in action for helping friends. He is not a mere sympathiser. But he is not that vocal in criticising friend decision, a god fearing person.

He did not say any thing to me as such .

Both of them came to Station to say me goodbye. Gave me an envelope with some money and said open this when u have nothing. Sounds filmy today ????

Train started moving. Slept without fear, a new journey. A new place.

In the after noon, I got down at New Delhi railway station. I had just a bolster, Ek round takia and a mat. And some clothes and book. I went to posh Defence Colony. There I found, I was given a wrong address. That man never stayed there. Chaukidar threw me out.

I still remember face of and his voice of chaukidar.

Music was going on in car. Again it was heavy rain. We had approached Delhi by pass .

I was recalling how well I had slept on railway station. A long story of big journey. A long path to discuss.

Yes I could achieve and became achiever just because of my approach of thinking all times in right approach and be positive .

What I stated doing have significant impact on social life. I think even if I am able to influence one percent of my participants then I will thank the almighty god for all ability he has given to me.

I thank god for every thing.

By this time I reached my home in Model Town. Watch man opened the door and car entered into a palatial house.

God does right all the time.

Conclusion

After going through above success stories, it is evident that nothing is impossible when one starts 'Thinking Positive'.

The only need is to remember the following Success Mantra:

DBCA : Your Dream, Commitment, Self-Belief makes the dream Achievable.

Late Dr A P J Abdul Kalam, Ex- President of India once remarked that dreams are those which are seen with the naked eyes. His meaning was to see those dream which you want to be realised.

Dreams to be SMART (Specific, Measurable, Achievable, Realisable and time based).

Merely seeing the dreams does not work in life till some of them are realised. One should not stop dreaming as it will stop progress of self ,society and nation. Richard Nixon,the president of USA, saw a big dream to send the astronauts to Moon. Apollo-II was the spaceflight that landed the first two humans on the Moon. Mission commander Neil Armstrong and pilot Buzz Aldrin, both Americans, landed the lunar module Eagle on July 20, 1969.

To dream is essential for human life, but the major issue is its realisation thereof. Commitments and Self- Belief makes the dream achievable.

Commitment: It has got inherent inspirational power, which defines the mental level of the individual towards a particular objective. It is better to have self-commitment towards yourself so that no one should follow it. It is willingness to give your time and energy to something that you believe in, or a promise or firm decision to do something. Most of our dreams were not realised due to lack of commitment. One should not leave the objective in between due to hurdles or barriers. You commitments drive you to cross the barriers. Fulfilling commitments may take lot of energy, but it is definite one of the key ingredients to success.

Self- Belief

It is the most important attribute for dream realisation. Self belief should be like that of Edmond Hillary's.

When he could not rise to the Everest in his first attempt, he said,

"Mount Everest, you beat me the first time, but I'll beat you the next time because you've grown all you are going to grow...but I'm still growing.

That was his belief in self.

During the Everest expedition, which was first of its kind, Sir Edmund Hillary's narrated inspiring these words:

- No one remembers who climbed Mount Everest the second time.
- You don't have to be intellectually bright to be a competent leader.
- As a youngster I was a great dreamer, reading many books of adventure and walking lonely miles with my head in the clouds.
- You don't have to be a hero to accomplish great things—to compete. You can just be an ordinary chap, sufficiently motivated to reach challenging goals.
- People do not decide to become extraordinary. They decide to accomplish extraordinary things.
- I have been seriously afraid at times but have used my fear as a stimulating factor rather than allowing it to paralyse me. My abilities have not been outstanding, but I have had sufficient strength and determination to meet my challenges and have usually managed to succeed with them.
- Life's a bit like mountaineering – never look down.
- While on top of Everest, I looked across the valley towards the great peak Makalu and mentally worked

out a route about how it could be climbed. It showed me that even though I was standing on top of the world, it wasn't the end of everything. I was still looking beyond to other interesting challenges.

- It is not the mountain we conquer, but ourselves.

Lets read another anecdote

Long ago, there was a battle about to take place. One of the generals was talking about tactics with his team of officers. An officer interrupted him and explained that he thought that the strategy was a waste of time.

"The gods have already decided who will win." he proclaimed.

"Are you suggesting that fate has decided the result in advance?" the general asked.

"Yes, I am." the officer responded.

The general took a coin out of his pocket and said, "So if I toss this coin and it comes up heads, we win, but if it's tails we lose. Is that how fate works?"

"Pretty much." said the officer. The general tossed the coin and it came up heads.

"See, the gods have decided. We can't lose now!"

They went to their troops with the good news and the soldiers marched into battle with renewed enthusiasm. After a glorious victory, the officers met in the general's tent to celebrate.

"Do you believe in fate now?" the general was asked.

The leader smiled, reached into his pocket and pulled out the coin to show to the others. It was heads on both sides.

"No, I don't believe in fate, just the value of self belief. When the soldiers thought that we couldn't lose, I knew that we couldn't lose."

Sometimes, we think that the script has been written and that success is for a chosen few.

I share this adapted story with you today to encourage you to believe in yourself, to have confidence in your abilities and to launch yourself into the fray with energy and enthusiasm. If you do, great victories will be won.

□

Notes

(I am being Positive)

Pen down your thoughts/experiences –

Takeaway –

6

My experiences on Positive thoughts

"Our greatest enemies, the ones we must fight most often, are within."

—Thomas Paine

My experiences on Positive thoughts

Below *Positive Thoughts* have been compiled to convey that they have a significant impact on life. They are the drivers of our spirit, which guides the way.

1. ***Ability*** without results is a disability. Ability to convert efforts, circumstances into desired results mark the culmination of **'Yes, I can'.**

It is one of the great skills, which is part of competence and also is the ability to recover from failure. Everyone fails in life, but a successful person shows a faster pace to return to normalcy.

In Mahabharata, Krishna told Arjun that although he had the ability, he was not using it constructively. It is like having the ability to work but it is of no use to the organisation; here it becomes a sheer disability. There is also a minor difference between skill and competence. Skill is the technique to do something and competence is the application of the same. If you are not able to apply your skills, you will be treated as incompetent. The winner is that person who is able to convert efforts and circumstances into the desired results. Krishna also told that effort is the vector quantity which should be given direction for its application. A person who can master this attribute has a greater chance of succeeding and saying, **'Yes, I can'.**

2. ***Aspire, Perspire and Inspire***: In life, whatever may be the circumstances, one needs to aspire and in order to have that, one has to perspire and after achieving the goals, one can inspire others to develop similar winning traits.

"If you can dream it, you can do it."

—Walt Disney Company

Aspiration is the first requirement to achieve success in life. I asked one of the officials in my company when he was around 35-years old as to what was his aspiration in life. He plainly replied that he wanted to reach the top management of the company. This is the first level of the journey, Krishna explained to Arjun, who asked for the fundamentals of success. He further advised that in order to succeed, aspirations have to be converted into results through perspiration. You need to slog for hours; work even at nights; leave home early; may have to cut time of family.

"Genius is 1% inspiration and 99% perspiration."

—Thomas A. Edison

Perspiration is the key ingredient for success. We generally envy the success of others but how much they have had to perspire to reach where they are, we are unable to see.

Success should not be confined to you but others too should be able to take advantage of the strategy and learning you developed in your journey from aspiration and perspiration to success. Be a role model and share your stories with others; you can even hand-hold others to success.

"In the long run, men only hit what they aim at. Therefore, though they may fail initially, they can better aim at something high."

—Henry David Thoreau

3. *Assume Positivity, Deny Negativity*: It is the key to success in life. Life is full of negativity; one needs to develop positivity and deny negativity because positivity alone can provide the direction to move ahead, whereas negativity takes one towards blame, criticism, delays, etc. Negative thoughts are like cactus, which does not allow positive thoughts to crop up.

One must learn to remain strong in a conflicting and disputing environment with the help of positive attitude and behavior.

When positive thoughts start penetrating the mind, negative memories from the subconscious also get erased as thoughts have the power to do so. If in reality, the mind starts having positive magnetism, negative memories will get erased and new and positive experiences will take their place. Experience it.

4. Be you own role model

Be your own role model, compete with yourself, raise your performance instead looking for other role models.

Peter Drucker, the great Management Guru has quoted, "If you can't measure it, you can't improve it."

We need to measure the performance with a benchmark.

Take the case of Usain bolt, the sprint runner. He always betters his performance. He competes with himself..

In the same way in our professional life also, do delta

betterment in ourselves by improving our attitude, behavior, competence in a measureable format and challenge our own performance.

"Measure what is measurable and make measurable what is not so."

—Galileo

As per above quote from great Galileo, we don't measure what is to be measured and measure what is not so important.

Most of the time we forget measuring our own performance and allow other to measure it.

Develop our achievement targets, deliberately achieve them and measure it regularly. It would help in enhancing your own efficiency enabling you to be your own role model.

5. ***Barriers & Constraints***: Barriers are opportunities for a fighter to overcome them. Barriers should excite you to overcome them. Fight till the last minute. Winners possess this prime attribute and believe in 'never say die'. Try it, experiment with it and enhance your success index.

Constraints are detrimental to progress and in particular, considering the time at disposal. Better to identify the gross and net constraints to be resolved on a monthly basis and not shove them under the carpet. Gross constraints are total constraints as on date, whereas net constraints are those which are not in your control. Earmark a day of the month and turn the mind to the solution of these constraints.

Control Reaction Points: Identify the points on which you react: time delay, traffic, people not working as per requirement, lack of governance, etc. Analyse every day and identify your points of reactions. Develop an action plan to avoid impulsive reactions which can be detrimental. To counter impulsive reactions, one technique is to close the fist and take three long breaths. Try it.

You cannot change the environment but can definitely change the reaction to a situation. Before reacting to a situation, think twice on your response to check whether it is required at the moment or not. It is like changing the habit and has a tremendous impact when you rise on the professional ladder. Observe it.

6. 4Ds: The desire to deliver results is more important than any other attribute. Follow the 4ds: dream, desire, develop and deliver.

It is the right of every individual to dream. Hope and optimism are helpful in realising your dream. Start dreaming and take it to fulfillment with hope and optimism.

Most dreams get shattered when they do not get fulfilled. The proper cycle of dream realisation is:

- ***Dream***: Better to have a realistic dream to start with. However, after the realisation of small dreams, bigger dreams can be envisaged. We all desire to achieve. Calculate the ratio of achievements and dreams to obtain the success quotient. For being rated as a successful person, the ratio should be more than 0.85.
- ***Desire*** is an essential component before realisation. One may have dreams, but if the desire is not there, no dream can reach realisation.
- ***Develop***: Next step is to develop the dream realisation sequence. Development of a strategy and action plan helps in the realisation of the dream.
- ***Delivery***: It is the ultimate step in fulfilling the dream.

Your Dream, Commitment towards the objective and Belief in self, make the dream Achievable.

7. Delta

- ***Delta Change***: In one of the cricket matches, Indian cricketer Bhumra slightly changed the style of bowling and got wickets. In the same way, try to do delta change in self to acquire more productivity. A slight change in habits and thinking can make a significant improvement.
- Self-improvement is an assessment with an action plan for enhancing the content level as per the requirement of the environment. It is better to develop one good habit every year as part of Delta improvement, i.e. a small step towards improvement.

8. Diya-*Baati Syndrome*: In Indian temples, people light the lamp with oil in a container (*Diya*) and a thick cotton thread (*baati*) is lit to pray to god. This has an analogy in life – till the oil is there in the *diya*, the *baati* would burn and light up the area, and as soon as the oil level falls, the *baati* too gets burnt totally and it no longer exists. In the same way, we all are like the *baati* which burns itself to give light to all, so long as we possess internal and external motivation. However, to give sustained light, it is better to have an internal motivation to be able to provide a consistent supply of motivation.

Similarly, in an organisational structure, the organisation *baatis* are its employees. The lamp shape where the *baati* is placed is the organisation and the oil is the eco-system of the organisation. As long as the eco-system of the organisation is sufficient to feed the employee, the employee will burn from the tip and give light in the form of productivity and efficiency.

There are thousands of employees working in different organisations. Strong management is required to develop an inspiring and motivational eco-system to enable the *baati* to light forever and contribute to its success.

9. *Execution Excellence*: In football or hockey, one player makes a pass for others to make a goal but it is the person who scores the goal who is remembered. In life also, we generally make a pass for others to execute. You can also make a goal when you can create a condition to convert the goal. Thus, train yourself with competence in executing. Develop a passion for excelling.

Everyone has got an Everest (highest mountain peak in the world) to conquer, a Hanuman to discover and a Ravana to destroy.

- ***Everest***: A goal to achieve, which one needs to internalise. Identify the same and aspire and reach the Everest.
- ***Hanuman***: In the epic *Ramayana*, Hanuman was blessed with tremendous power. All that was required was to make him realise his dormant power. Similarly, internal power/energy needs to be discovered within because each of us has tremendous power lying dormant within us.
- ***Ravana*** was a demon in the epic *Ramayana* to boast that none could defeat him. This pride in his power (negative thinking) was the real cause of his downfall and led to the destruction of his kingdom in Sri Lanka. We need to identify all such weaknesses which contribute to our failures.

10 *Failure & Fatigue*: Failure is a prelude to success and this is something that one tends to overlook. Successful people are equally concerned about their failure and their accomplishments. Being successful is a crucial aspect of life. Note down the number of times you have failed to reach your goal. It is advisable to undertake this exercise every month and self-introspect.

Failure is the starting point of success. Review your strategy and action plan and try again and again till you get the desired objective.

Failure should not deter me and being successful and maintaining success is a difficult task in comparison to failure. After every failure, success shall come. So be hopeful after every defeat.

Failure is bound to happen but it is more important to realise how soon you can overcome it and bounce back to normal. Failures are stepping stones to success. In fact, the word 'failure' should be deleted from the dictionary of life since it casts an adverse psychological impact.

Failure is something that people hesitate to talk and discuss as they have a psychological impact. However, it is better to discuss, say in the mid of every month and identify the reasons for the same. Failures are accepted but failing on the same point time, again and again, is not welcome.

Fatigue: In this competitive life:

'Life is a marathon
Fatigue and stoppage are not allowed.
Get up, walk, run, fall down, again get up or crawl,
Don't stop till you reach the goal.'

11. Goal

- The goals from a distance appear hazy and it becomes difficult for us to concentrate on them. It is better to break the goals into smaller or shorter goals to acquire better visibility to reach them and accordingly the efforts get directed towards the same.
- Goals are made in life to achieve them and in order to reach them, one needs to take micro-steps every day and advance gradually towards the goal.

- They can be achieved only when we move towards the same. One step every day would take you nearer to the goal. Remember just one step a day is enough. Try it.

DBO: Delivery by objective is the key to success in professional life. Always understand the objective or goal and direct your experience, knowledge, competence, and energy towards the same to enhance the probability to succeed. Try it.

12. Happiness

- Don't postpone your happiness. Satisfaction is your birthright. No one can snatch it until you allow it. So celebrate the moments of joy, feel and share them.
- Let happiness become a habit which emanates from behavior change. Search for happiness within your inner self and experience the same.
- People and circumstances may disturb you, but you need to control yourself as you and only you can control yourself. It would enhance your happiness throughout the day.
- It is a state of mind, which is in your control. Thus control the mind from ingress of negative thoughts and remain happy as far as possible. Happiness is in your hand.
- It is a function of time. It is a state of contentment within oneself and in order to obtain sustainable happiness, one needs to sweat to realise one's aspirations.
- Think of the happy instances to come out of negativity and be happy, instead of being unhappy. Happy thoughts early in the morning drive away from the negatives and keep you happy the whole day. Sleeping with happy thoughts helps in deciding the course of life. Try it.

The night is connected with the day with hardwire, i.e. the

day follows the night. Similarly, bad days are hard-wired with good ones, so do not feel depressed in adverse situations because happy days are on the anvil.

13. Hope: One day, my son slept till late in the morning. I told him, "Get up, my son; a new day has begun, bringing in a lot of hope and possibilities. New sunshine is there; darkness is over. Get up, my son, a new day has begun." In fact, every day is a new day, full of hope and inspiration. It is better to be hopeful every day.

The first thought in the morning on getting up drives and determines your day. Recall an inspiring event or feeling. Develop the habit of positive imagery for being successful. Positive thoughts emerge from the subconscious mind. Thus it is advisable to have happy and inspiring moments stored in the subconscious mind to remain pepped up in the day.

14. *Intrinsic and Extrinsic Inspiration*: Every day, we have to struggle against our circumstances, making it difficult for us to get extrinsic inspiration, that is, from others as everyone is fighting his or her own battle. It is better to have one's own inspiration inventory to get intrinsically inspired to face the circumstances and be a winner.

We should develop an inventory of inspiring events, thoughts, stories, etc. related to our lives so as to invoke them immediately at the time of troublesome situations.

In order to be happy, one should get over one's painful points. This can be done by developing one's own pain-killers through internal inspiration.

Take time out to get connected with the inner self and with inner thoughts. Be the observer of thoughts, their quality, and quantity. Positive auto-suggestions prove beneficial.

15. Life

- It is a function of accumulated goals which we reconcile at the end of our professional age. Long-distant goals are hazy as they are not on the line of sight, so it is better to break goals into small goals, which is easy to achieve.
- It is like sailing a boat from one end to another. We are sailors with the competence to take the boat of life from one end to another under different circumstances, including storms, disturbances, etc.
- *Life is nothing but a journey of patience, pursuance, and perseverance.* These qualities make for the significant differences between a successful and an unsuccessful person. A successful person makes effective and efficient utilisation of time.
- Try to drive the car of your *life* in different gears and according to the speed, change the gear, i.e. 'change the attitude, etc. of your life to reach your destination safely.'

Life Success Quotient (LSQ) depends on your achievements, which in turn depend upon the utilisation of time. Identify time-wasters and make efficient use of time to have better LSQ (around 60 years of age when living in the present). In life, there are two days, yesterday and today. *Enjoy today with color and spirit and learn from yesterday.*

16. *Learning*: Life is a summation of days. The journey from Monday to Sunday has been changed to a day instead of a week. Throughout the day we work and the outcome of the day is as below:

Outcome of the day = Work done + Experience + Learning

Work done is visible whereas experience is invisible as it goes to the subconscious level of the mind. But the learning component is the deliberate aspect which could help in making a man more productive the next day.

Successful persons have one of the significant attributes of learning from any event at all. It is better to recall the daily learning situations before sleeping and enhancing your net balance of learning as it will enable you to enrich your knowledge day by day.

Let us be more prosperous by acquiring at least one aspect of information every day and ponder over its annual impact.

Think of a situation when you have at least 100 learning situations in a year. These would enhance the richness of your life in terms of knowledge, which sharpens the sword of experience.

17. *Lock and Key*: People have the habit of getting scared of locks or barriers in professional life. As a principle, every lock has to have the key to open, so it is better to work on essentials like the keys rather than on locks.

It has been seen that during the course of one's work, one gets entangled in issues which one views as roadblocks and locks. This develops negativity in one.

Thus after seeing the locks and roadblocks, better start thinking of solutions to open the lock or cross the barriers. Thinking Positive, if practiced adequately, is able to convert the thought process.

18 *Mind*: Don't allow others to hack your brain. You and only you are the controllers, so control your mind and regulate your self.

Train the mind with positive thoughts and regular practice would develop a subconscious positive field in the mind. This would keep you inspired even during adverse periods. It may act like a firewall, which will not allow any negative thought to creep in.

Instead of changing the mindset, develop the mind, open the mind, enhance your ROM (Random Only Memory, a term used in computer science to denote permanent memory of the system, which cannot be erased) to accommodate positive thoughts so that whenever negative thoughts arise, positive thinking will arise from ROM to eliminate the negative thoughts.

19. Optimism

- ***Optimism, Realism, and Pessimism***: One can be at any of the three stages. Challenge is to be at the mid-level, so better be at the optimal level. Optimism can be converted to realism through timely action.
- Arise every morning with hope and sleep at night with a pleasant dream. Hope and optimism are helpful in realising your dream. Start dreaming and take it to fulfillment through hope and optimism.
- These attributes are present in all the winners. They keep on winning on account of optimism and these become a part of their life-like breath.

20. Outliers

- When you climb the snow-covered mountain, an avalanche of snow slides down and breaks your momentum. This is the inflection point which requires deft handling. Attributes like courage, passion, and obstinacy towards the objective would help you to face it and emerge as an outlier. Visualise and feel it.
- A positive outlier is a person who goes beyond plateaus and makes the impossible possible. For such people, the objective and cause are supreme. All mental and physical attributes align with the goal.

- Outliers have aspirations which enable them to make the impossible possible. Don't allow aspirations to die. They are the fuel to the life engine which you are driving. Keep on aspiring.

Success Recipe: One may have skills but not the speed and stamina. The synchronisation of skills, speed and stamina lead one to the road of success.

21. *Problem Solving*: Incubate the problem in such a way and till such a time that robust solutions come out.

In fact, the problem exists until the time we find the solution. All the problems have the seed to solution. Problems and solutions are like day and night. Either we don't see the solution, or we don't want to solve the problem.

Problems are like googlies or bouncers in cricket parlance. At start one ducks but later on, develops the skill of playing the bouncers. Our life is similar. One is required to acquire the skill to either duck or play under these circumstances; otherwise, one would be retired hurt or caught behind. Thus always be agile to unlearn, learn and relearn.

It becomes easier when self-emotions are taken out of problems. Emotions develop a negative eco-environment for solving the problem. It is advisable to detach oneself and come out of it; the solution will emerge automatically. Experiment with this.

22. Relationship

- It is like a chemical reaction between two elements. The chemical reaction's efficiency depends on elements reacting with each other. Relationship chemistry needs proper temperature and pressure conditions to bring about any chemical reaction.

- ***Connect is like Co-valent Bond*** :Any sustainable connectivity is like a covalent bond, a term used in chemistry, where two atoms are connected with each other tightly. A similar analogy could be applied to the relationship. It should be so strong that no amount of external pressure can break it.'
- Human relationships are complex and one of the arch pillars is the perception of the individual. Stable and sustainable relationship seeks sincerity, credibility, and trustworthiness among the members who are entering into a relationship.
- In a relationship, one member has to be at the lower potential for a regular flow of current. If the potential is the same, there will not be any flow of current. Further, there has to be no resistance in between, else the flow of the current would get restricted.

23. Self-development

- You are a product which should have sale-able properties. So plan for continuous self-development by reading, learning and sharing to develop yourself. Take out a minimum of two hours for yourself to acquire attributes as per the requirements of the profession.
- ***Self-assessment, Self-improvement, Self-development***: A positive person works for continuous betterment through assessment of strengths and weaknesses and working for constant development in order to work with others.

Shape Yourself: As we go to the gym to shape our body, similarly shape yourself with a positive approach, patience, empathy, and knowledge.

Take out a minimum of one hour a day for self – physical, mental and spiritual development. For starters, start reading developmental books and witness changes in your personality within 21 days.

Take lessons from the past, live today and prepare for the future.

The win is like a thrill; feel that thrill.

24. Success

- Success is nothing but betterment of failures. Failures teach us to become better. Application of learning in acts inches us towards success.
- Success not only needs to be cherished but also to be analysed for future success.
- Reaching up to 'can do' may take 50 % time. It is a success point from this point. Success journey starts and one never looks back. Thus find more time to make yourself ready till success point.
- Success does not see any caste, creed or color. It is the yield of your aspiration, perspiration, and perseverance.
- The sweetness of success increases when it comes after overcoming adverse or opposite circumstances.
- In order to get success, you must have a clear goal, strategy, action plan, execution, and perseverance.
- For success in any venture, one is required to convert probability to a possibility, develop strategy and action plan and execute to get the desired delivery. Try it.

Success Attributes: Everyone strives for success in their field. One of the key attributes for success is your staying power with the problem before the solution. One has to stand firm, irrespective of circumstances.

Success Mantra

- Based on experience, it is concluded that some of the attributes leading to success in life are simplicity, sincerity, and serenity of the mind.
- Think positive, think possible, think options and think solutions. Empower yourself with desired competence and realise, 'Yes, I can and yes, I will'.
- Since it is difficult to succeed alone, it is better to follow 4cs: convergence, co-existence, corporation, and collaboration. They are vital parameters for success in today's world.

25. Time

- Time is a function of desire, i.e. one takes out time for the work which one wants to do. Ignite the passion/ desire with this objective.
- Time and team are essential constituents of life.
- Time is the most precious commodity. Keep an account of every hour. If in leisure, germinate positive thoughts, which will transform you to acquire better efficiency. *Wastage of time is more than crime as it is irreversible.*
- Tomorrow never comes in this complex world; life is for two days – yesterday and today. Yesterday is for learning and today is for the use of knowledge and execution of plan. Use your time effectively
- Use your time efficiently either by thinking or by actions for self (25 %), organisation (50 %) and society (25 %). All aspects of life should be included in your attention inventory.
- ***Time Efficiency***: Every minute leaves us with tick-tick sound. Success depends upon the effective utilisation of our time. Calculate the daily time efficiency as active

time utilised and ensure it more than 80 % to acquire sustainable success.

26. Team

- It is nothing but a chain integrating all components and sub-components.
- In order to get performance, the minds of the team have to have neuro-connection or alignment with the objective.
- TEAM – Together, Engaging and Motivating.
- The sweetness of success increases when it comes after overcoming adverse or opposing circumstances.
- It is nothing but a combination of photons (packet of energy) if joined together to produce tremendous power to destroy the enemy in the form of obstructions, on the way to the goal.

27. Yes, I can

- Win over 3 Fs: fear, failure, and frustration, which are detrimental to progress in life and can be countered by a thought 'yes, I can'.
- *Yes, I can and One more Effort towards the Goal* Never say 'no', till the goal is accomplished.
- '*Yes, I can'* is nothing but a feeling of self-realisation and understanding of one's strength and empowering self to reach the desired goal in different phases of life.
- '*Yes, I can*' is a powerful word. Chant it over breakfast and before sleeping. Try it on your children and see the change in their performances.

□

Notes

(I am being Positive)

Pen down your thoughts/experiences –

Takeaway –

7

Our Vision on Positivity

"A time has come to develop Generation (P3) i.e. Positive, Proactive & Progressive required for sustainable development of the country."

—Dr. Ashutosh Karnatak

Our Vision on Positivity

Apart from developing and inculcating a sense of Positive Self in individuals, the bigger aim is to foster Positivity in different aspects of life.

Positive Eco-System:

Transformation is not easy. It has been mentioned that it is like changing the wheel of a running vehicle .Most of the transformation fails due to implementation with lack of mental preparation of the society. Any transformation or change is possible when all the people are mentally ready for the same .It is, in today's term, called preparation of the **"Eco-System."** It could be easily understood by **"Gardener Theory."**

Gardener Theory: Gardner is a person who before sowing the seed, prepares the soil suitable for the seed. We get happy after getting the final product - fruit, but the gardener has to do a lot before getting the result .His steps are:

- **Checking the suitability of the soil**
- **Preparation of the field**
- **Putting the desired manure and mixing it with the soil**
- **Putting the adequate water**
- **Getting a seed which could produce**

- **Sowing the seed**
- **Nurturing the plant till it gains its strength**
- **Weeding out the trash, which is detrimental to the growth. It is one of the significant actions taken by the gardener.**

In the same way, should one want to transform Self, Society ,Country or the World, he has to develop a Positive Eco –System like a Gardener should have sufficient and sustainable soil and surrounding eco-system.

- **Sustainability through Positive thinking**
- **Helping each other & Collaborating**
- **Smiling**
- **Can do" Approach**
- **Try and try again**
- **Achiever & Winning approach**
- **Positive Approach: working for solutions.**

Thus, Develop an Eco-System before any change or Transformation.

Positive Home

Home is the first place of learning even before taking birth. When the child is conceived, the eco-system of the house is inherited by the child being at the womb. It is all the more necessary to have Positive, Inspiring and Happy eco-system at home before and after birth.

Based on the experience, following elements are part of Positive Home:

1. **Happy atmosphere in the home**
2. **A loving and caring approach**
3. **Always ready to help each other**
4. **Respect for elders and love for younger**
5. **Calm and positive environment**

6. **Trust and cooperation amongst family members**
7. **Thinking positive (All is well approach)**

Thus, Develop a Positive Home for self and the family.

Positive Life partner

Life partner is one of the most talked about subject. Most of the people have to pass through the ritual of marriage and consequent upon it the concept of life partner emerges. Our motivation in life largely depends upon the relationship with the life partner. So, how is the positive life partner :

1. **One who is happy**
2. **One who cares**
3. **One who understands**
4. **One who is trustworthy**
5. **One who is transparent in communication**
6. **One who is supportive**
7. **One who is always willing to share responsibilities**

Develop characteristics of a Positive Life Partner to lead a happy and peaceful married life.

Positive Professional

Professional life is a journey from the day you enter and exit. This journey is full of ups and downs, full of learnings, professional storms & typhoons, traps, etc. The person who comes out clearly & safely is the real winner. Some of the personal break down in this journey, however, some face the situations boldly with courage & conviction

Positivity is not a concept but a reality, which is required to be adopted by professional to be successful. Some of the attributes which are of High impact and high Importance are:

1. **Positive Approach**
2. **Developing competence as per requirement**

3. **Having "Can-Do" approach**
4. **Good communicator (Verbal & Writing)**
5. **Smiling face**
6. **Unruffled despite problems or barriers**
7. **Helping Others**

Thus, Develop yourself as a Positive Professional to be progressive in life.

Positive Client :

In the professional life, the client has a significant role for the development of others. Many stakeholders are at the mercy of the same. At the organisation level, it is a client-stakeholder relationship the primary issue. Knowing well that it's a time of co-existence, the approach of clients need to be transformed.

1. **So, Positive Client means:**
2. **Caring for stakeholders**
3. **Positive approach**
4. **A good** listener to the stakeholder
5. **Hand holding the stakeholder**
6. **Giving feedback & Solution provider**
7. **Understanding and Coaching them**
8. **Inspiring them at the hour of need**

Better to develop ourselves as a good client.

"If you want to conquer fear, don't sit home and think about it. Go out and get busy."

—Dale Carnegie

Positive Customer

As told earlier we all are born positive, but on the way in the journey of life ,we mental disposition is adulterated towards negativity. Greed is one of the factors which influences the mind. The existence in the society is based on co-existence, and everyone is a customer for others. One has to give service whereas others have to receive the same with some terms and condition, which is called a contract. Positive approach keeps us in the bandwidth of `righteousness, Judicious, etc.

What a Positive Customer is :

1. **Having trust in the client/supplier**
2. **Complying the contract conditions**
3. **Positive Approach and behavior**
4. **Following the law of the land**
5. Belief on a quality product
6. **Concern about efficiency**
7. **Environment-friendly**

Be a Positive Customer....

Positive City

Positivity is a habit, behaviors, and culture. People living in cities also feel comfortable when cities have some attributes. Some of the Attributes by which the town is known and leads to develop **"Positive City."**

Some of the characteristics of such cities are:

1. **Cleanliness & Sanitation**
2. **Pollution free having blue sky**
3. **Wide roads also pit free**
4. **Full of trees and garden having colorful flowers**
5. **Harmony among people**
6. **Clean and Sufficient water**
7. **Poor being is taken care of**

We can have it if we think..... Let it be a dream but let us have an inspiring goal.

"The greatest discovery is that people can change their future simply by changing their attitude."

—Oprah Winfrey

□

Notes

(I am being Positive)

Pen down your thoughts/experiences –

Takeaway –

8

Inspiring Positive Quotes

Inspiring Positive Quotes

1. I have not failed. I have just found 10,000 things that do not work.' - Thomas Edison, 1847-1931
2. 'The brain is wider than the sky.' - Emily Dickinson, 1830-1886
3. 'Great spirits have often overcome violent opposition from mediocre minds.' - Albert Einstein, 1879-1955
4. 'We are so made that we can only derive intense enjoyment from contrast and only very little from the state of things.' - Sigmund Freud, 1856-1939
5. 'I am not bound to succeed, but I am bound to live up to what light I have.' - Abraham Lincoln, 1809-1865
6. 'Don't become a mere recorder of facts, but try to penetrate the mystery of their origin.' - Ivan Pavlov, 1849-1936
7. 'The habit of giving only enhances the desire to give.'- Walt Whitman
8. 'As we advance in life, we learn the limits of our abilities'- James A. Froude, 1818-1894, British historian
9. 'I know I have the ability to do so much more than just stand in front of the camera the rest of my life.' - Jennie Garth, 1972, American actress

10. 'We cannot restore integrity and morality to our society until each of us – singly and individually – takes responsibility for our actions.' - Harry Emerson Fosdick
11. 'Action on the move creates its own route; creates to a very great extent the conditions under which it is to be fulfilled and thus baffles all calculation.' - Henri Bergson
12. 'Adversity has the effect of eliciting talents which, in prosperous circumstances, would have lain dormant.' - Horace, 65-8 B.C.
13. 'The aim of an argument or discussion should not be victory, but progress.' - Joseph Joubert
14. 'What I must do is all that concerns me, not what the people think.' - Ralph Waldo Emerson
15. 'Trials, temptations, disappointments – all these help instead of hindrances if one uses them rightly. They not only test the fibre of a character but strengthen it. Every conquered temptation represents a new fund of moral energy. Every trial endured and weathered in the right spirit makes a soul nobler and stronger than it was before.' - James Buckham
16. 'Some men have thousands of reasons why they cannot do what they want to when all they need is one reason why they can.' - Mary Frances Berry
17. 'My motto was to keep swinging. Whether I was in a slump or feeling bad or having trouble off the field, the only thing to do was to keep swinging.' - Hank Aaron
18. 'A day spent without the sight or sound of beauty, the contemplation of mystery, or the search of truth or perfection is a poverty-stricken day; and a succession of such days is fatal to human life.' - Mumford Lewis, 1895-1990, American social philosopher

19. 'When (he) was asked from whom he learned better, he replied, 'From those without goodness, because what seemed unbecoming in them I avoid doing myself." - Sufi master
20. 'No one is any better than you, but you are no better than anyone else until you do something to prove it.'- Donald Laird
21. 'Before you can inspire with emotion, you must be swamped with it yourself. Before you can move their tears, your own must flow. To convince them, you must believe.' - Winston Churchill
22. 'Any change, even for the better, is always accompanied by drawbacks and discomforts.' - Arnold Bennett, 1867-1931, British novelist
23. 'Those who stand for nothing fall for anything.' - Alexander Hamilton
24. 'In judging character, too often we mistake rigidity for morality.' - Dero Ames Saunders
25. 'Some day, in years to come, you will be wrestling with the great temptation or trembling under the great sorrow of your life. But the real struggle is here, now, in these quiet weeks. Now it is being decided whether, in the day of your supreme sorrow or temptation, you shall miserably fail or gloriously conquer. A character cannot be made except by a steady, long, continued process.' - Phillips Brooks
26. 'The ultimate measure of a man is not where he stands in moments of comfort and convenience, but where he stands at times of challenge and controversy.' - Martin Luther King Jr.
27. 'Courage is about the management of fear, not the absence of fear.' - Rudy Giuliani

28. 'Each indecision brings its own delays and days are lost lamenting over lost days. What you can do or think you can do, begin it. For boldness has magic, power and genius in it.' - Johann Wolfgang von Goethe, 1749-1832, poet, novelist and scientist
29. 'Being defeated is often only a temporary condition. Giving up is what makes it permanent.' - Marilyn Vos Savant, 1946
30. 'Defeat is simply a signal to press onward.' - Helen Keller
31. 'You can't push anyone up the ladder unless he is willing to climb himself.' - Andrew Carnegie
32. 'Excellence is an art won by training and habituation. We do not act rightly because we have virtue or excellence, but rather we have those because we have acted rightly. We are what we repeatedly do. Excellence, then, is not an act but a habit.' - Aristotle
33. 'Before you can inspire with emotion, you must be swamped with it yourself. Before you can move their tears, your own must flow. To convince them, you must believe.' - Winston Churchill
34. 'When a father gives to his son, both laugh; when a son gives to his father, both cry.' - Jewish proverb
35. 'Somewhere, something incredible is waiting to be known.' - Carl Sagan, astronomer
36. 'It is no use saying, "We are doing our best." You have got to succeed in doing what is necessary.' - Winston Churchill, British statesman
37. 'Always make a total effort, even when the odds are against you.' - Arnold Palmer, golfer
38. 'We must walk consciously only part way towards our goal and then a leap in the dark to our success.' - Henry David Thoreau

39. 'Ah, but a man's reach should exceed his grasp, or what's a heaven for?' - Robert Browning
40. 'Big goals get big results. No goals get no results or somebody else's results.' - Mark Victor Hansen
41. 'It is not enough to be industrious; so are the ants. What are you industrious about?' - James Thurber
42. 'He who has a way to live for can bear almost anyhow.'- Friedrich Nietzsche
43. 'We all have something to give. So if you know how to read, find someone who can't. If you've got a hammer, find a nail. If you're not hungry, not lonely, not in trouble – seek out someone who is.' - George H.W. Bush
44. 'Even a small star shines in the darkness.' - Finnish proverb
45. 'I want to be thoroughly used up when I die, for the harder I work the more I love. I rejoice in life for its own sake. Life is no brief candle to me; it is a sort of splendid torch which I've got a hold of for the moment and I want to make it burn as brightly as possible before handing it on to future generations.' - George Bernard Shaw
46. 'If you want others to be happy, practice compassion. If you want to be happy, practice compassion.' - Dalai Lama
47. 'The ultimate test of man's conscience may be his willingness to sacrifice something today for future generations, whose words of thanks will not be heard.' - Gaylord Nelson
48. 'The ideals which have lighted my way, and time have given me new courage to face life cheerfully, are kindness, beauty, and truth.' - Albert Einstein
49. 'The natural fights of the human mind are not from pleasure to pleasure but from hope to hope.' - Samuel Johnson

50. 'A leader takes people where they want to go. A great leader takes people where they don't necessarily want to go, but ought to be.' - Rosalynn Carter
51. 'There are two ways of spreading light; to be the candle or the mirror reflecting it.' - Edith Wharton
52. 'The supreme happiness of life is the conviction that one is loved; loved for oneself, or better yet, loved despite oneself.' - Victor Hugo
53. 'The people who get on in this world are the people who get up and look for the circumstances they want, and if they cannot find them, make them.' - George Bernard Shaw
54. 'The fault is not in our stars, but in ourselves.' - Shakespeare
55. 'Though we travel the world over to find the beautiful, we must carry it with us, or we find it not.' - Ralph Waldo Emerson
56. 'When I was 15, I had underwear. When that failed, I had a lucky hairdo, then a lucky race number, even lucky race days. After 15 years, I've found the secret to success is simple. It's hard work.' - Margaret Groos
57. 'Duty is a very personal thing. It is what comes from knowing the need to take action and not just a need to urge others to do something.' - Mother Teresa
58. 'I don't wait for moods. You accomplish nothing if you do that. Your mind must know it has got to get down to work.' - Pearl S. Buck
59. 'What you can do, or dream you can, begin it. Boldness has genius, power, and magic in it.' - Goethe
60. 'A ship in harbour is safe – but that is not what ships are for.' - John A. Shedd.

61. 'If bravery is a quality which knows not fear, I have never seen a brave man. All men are frightened. The more intelligent they are, the more they are frightened. The courageous man is who forces himself, in spite of his fear, to carry on.' - General George S. Patton, Jr
62. 'Even when I was in the orphanage, when I was roaming the street trying to find enough to eat, even then I thought of myself as the greatest actor in the world. I had to feel the exuberance that comes from utter confidence in yourself. Without it, you go down to defeat.' - Charlie Chaplin
63. 'Discipline without freedom is tyranny; freedom without discipline is chaos.' - Cullen Hightower
64. 'A habit is like old-fashioned adhesive tape – easy to stick on, but the longer it stays, the harder it is to get off, until finally when it's ripped off; it takes skin and all with it.' - Sydney J. Harris
65. 'Moral excellence comes about as a result of habit. We become just by doing just acts, temperate by doing temperate acts, brave by doing brave acts.' - Aristotle
66. 'In mathematics, an integer is a number that isn't divided into factions. Just so, a man of integrity isn't divided against himself. He doesn't think one thing and say another – so he's not in conflict with his own principles.' - Arthur Gordon
67. 'The way to gain a good reputation is to endeavour to be what you desire to appear.' - Socrates
68. 'The time is always right to do what is right.' - Martin Luther King Jr.
69. 'The reputation of thousand years may be determined by the conduct of one hour.' - Japanese proverb

70. 'Be sure you've put your feet in the right place and then stand firm.' - Abraham Lincoln
71. 'I desire to so conduct the affairs of this administration that if, in the end, when I come to lay down the reins of power, I have lost every other friend on earth. I shall have at least one friend left – and that friend shall be down inside me.' - Abraham Lincoln
72. 'I wish parents would understand that if their child drops eight fly balls one day, then only drops six the next, that's a reason to go to Fairy Queen. The principal thing is competing against yourself. It's about self-improvement, about being better than you were the day before.' - Steve Young
73. 'Determine that the thing can and shall be done and then we shall find the way.' - Abraham Lincoln
74. 'Peak performers want more than merely to win the next game. They see all the way to the championship. They have a long-range goal that inspires commitment and action.' - Charles A. Garfield
75. 'The trouble with not having a goal is that you can spend your life running up and down the field and never scoring.' - Bill Copeland
76. 'The long-run men hit only what they aim at.' - Henry David Thoreau
77. 'The world is moved not only by the mighty shoves of the heroes but also by the aggregate of the tiny pushes of each honest worker.' - Helen Keller
78. 'If you can't feed a hundred people, then feed just one.' - Mother Teresa
79. 'Dig a well before you are thirsty.' - Chinese proverb
80. 'The will to win is not nearly as important as the will to prepare to win.' - Bobby Knight

81. 'Discovery consists of seeing what everybody has seen and thinking what nobody has thought.' - Albert Szent-Gyorgyi
82. 'Doing your best at this moment puts you in the best place for the next moment.' - Oprah Winfrey
83. 'The work praises the man.' - Irish proverb
84. 'Action may not always be happiness, but there is no happiness without action.' - Benjamin Disraeli
85. 'Few things help an individual more than to place responsibility upon him and to let him know that you must trust him.' - Booker T. Washington
86. 'Coming together is a beginning; keeping together is progress; working together is success.' - Henry Ford
87. 'Husband and wives complete themselves through each other, and the whole of the union becomes stronger and more wonderful than the sum of the two parts.' - William J. Bennett
88. 'Although the world is full of suffering, it is also full of the overcoming of it.' - Helen Keller
89. 'Adversity causes some men to break, others to break records.' - William Arthur Ward
90. 'The gem cannot be polished without friction.' - Chinese proverb
91. 'Wherever we look upon this earth, the opportunities take shape within the problems.' - Nelson A. Rockefeller
92. 'Anyone become angry. That is easy. But to be angry with the right person, to the right degree, at the right time, for the right purpose and in the right way – that is not easy.' - Aristotle
93. 'The greatest remedy for anger is a delay.' - Seneca
94. 'Every man should keep a fair-sized cemetery in which to bury the faults of his friends.' - Henry Ward Beecher

95. 'Fall seven times, stand up eight.' - Japanese proverb
96. 'You may have to fight a battle more than once to win it.' - Margaret Thatcher
97. 'Patience is a necessary ingredient of genius.' - Benjamin Disraeli
98. 'I had no special sagacity – only the power of patient thought.' - Sir Isaac Newton
99. 'Lose an hour in the morning, and you will be looking for it the rest of the day.' - Lord Chesterfield
100. 'Most time is wasted in minutes, not hours. The average person diddles away enough minutes in ten years to have earned a college degree.' - Dale Turner
101. 'Look to this day
For yesterday is but a dream,
And tomorrow is only a vision,
But today, well-lived,
Makes every yesterday a dream of happiness
And every tomorrow a vision of hope.
Look well, therefore, to this day.'

□□□

Notes

Write down points of transformation:

1. ....

2. ....

3. ....

4. ....

5. ....

6. ....

7. ....

8. ....

9. ....

10. ....

Notes

Notes

Finally, a Dedication

First and foremost, I thank my readers who over the years have encouraged me to continue with my passion of writing and pen down my experiences in the form of this book.

I would like to mention a few people who inspired me and made a significant contribution in turning my thought process into a book. These include my associates at Plus Approach Foundation, my colleagues at GAIL India Limited and all who have contributed by sharing their personal experiences. I am really thankful to all of them for their inputs and influence in shaping up this literary work.

My gratitude to the publisher, for enabling me to bring this book to all of you.

Last but not the least, to my dear wife and sons, Tanay & Pranay who are the guiding force for me to stay positive and motivating me to disseminate my thoughts and experiences through this book.